William Henry Denham Rouse

Tales from the isles of Greece

William Henry Denham Rouse

Tales from the isles of Greece

ISBN/EAN: 9783744730761

Printed in Europe, USA, Canada, Australia, Japan

Cover: Foto ©Andreas Hilbeck / pixelio.de

More available books at **www.hansebooks.com**

TALES FROM THE ISLES OF GREECE

A Greek Peasant.

TALES FROM THE ISLES
OF GREECE BEING SKETCHES
OF MODERN GREEK PEASANT
LIFE TRANSLATED FROM THE GREEK
OF ARGYRIS EPHTALIOTIS BY
W. H. D. ROUSE

LONDON MDCCCXCVII PUBLISHED BY
J. M. DENT & CO. ALDINE HOUSE E.C.
AND 67 SAINT JAMES'S STREET S.W.

Dedication

Herald of morn, when still the night was deep,
　Mother of heroes, nurse of arts divine,
Now newly wakened from millennial sleep,
　Hellas ! to thee whatever here is mine.

Ἑλλάς, σοὶ τόδε κεῖται, ἐπεί ποτε μούνη ἔλαμπες
　φῶς μαντευομένη νυκτερινῷ σκότεϊ,
ἡρώων μῆτερ, θείων μουσοτρόφε τεχνῶν,
　νῦν δ' ἀπὸ χιλιετοῦς ὕπνου ἐγειρομένη.

THE stories here offered to English readers are taken from a little book which has excited much interest in Greece. It is one of the few books dealing with their own peasant life that the Greeks of to-day have given us. With material so plentiful, and of such interest not only for themselves but for all who love Greece, we can only wonder and regret that there are so few books of the kind. One or two of the sketches in the original work have been omitted, and their place has been taken by three others given at the end, dealing with the days of the War of Independence. These have not yet been published, and have been translated from the author's manuscript. If among those that have been retained some are but slight, there is none but throws light upon the life and customs of the Greek peasant.

CONTENTS

IN THE GREEK ISLANDS

THERE is something Homeric still lingering about rural Greece, and especially about those isles of the Ægean where few travellers come. It is not only the delicate and voluble speech, which in spite of all its changes still suggests the ripple of the hexameter, if not its majesty; but the very life and thoughts of the people go back to an immemorial antiquity. On every barren hill an Eumæus in his μάνδρα, with fierce belling hounds that know each stranger for an enemy; Odysseus sailing the seas in a bark no other than those we see upon a Greek vase, its bows painted with just such a pair of huge eyes as of yore; Penelope weaving at her hand-loom, linen, or a carpet of bright colours; the same simple fare, the same open hospitality; Nereids haunting the brooks and the hills, Charon calling away the dead. It is not so long since blind Homers trudged the country side, and in return for a welcome, sang the heroic ballads of olden days; only now no Troy was their theme, but the struggle of Greece for freedom against the Turk.

Your host comes to his door to bid you welcome.

You enter the building, blind walls without, but within, rooms opening upon a courtyard, with perhaps a kind of verandah on the side. In the porch, basin and towel are brought you, and a son or daughter of the house pours water upon your hands. You take your seat on a stool or lounge, and the goodwife with her own hands brings in a tray of sweetmeats — a small glass of delicious jam, of which you take one spoonful, wishing the lady health in a set formula, to which she replies. Then follows the meal, the women waiting on you and your host; and finally mastick is brought on in little bottles, with grapes and figs or melons ; a dependent, half servant, half friend, of the same kin as your host, pours out continual drams of this potent spirit, of which he too is now and then permitted to taste. He sits in a corner, joins deferentially in the conversation ; while without, lounge one or two humbler servants, listening to all that goes on. Your host has a full share of curiosity, and will know who you are, where you live, your income, whether you have a wife, if not why not, all about you in short ; and equally ready to tell of himself. While you will, you are welcome to stay ; and as a rule there is no thought of payment. Even the poor will often make you their guest. On one occasion—and this not far from

Athens—I hired a man and mule for half a day.
After some little bargaining, we settled the price at
three drachmas, then worth something less than
eighteen pence. The bargain sealed by a sip of
sour wine, he said, "Where do you eat bread?"
"Oh," I said, "here, I suppose" (in the coffee-house).
"Come and eat with me," he answered. So I joined
my muleteer at his breakfast, where we had simple
fare, it is true, but plenty and hospitably offered :
salt fish, bread, cheese, wine of a sort, figs, grapes,
set on a wooden tray, while we reclined on the
floor ; and grace said by the priest long enough for
a Lord Mayor's banquet. On returning from my
excursion, he insisted on my sharing another meal,
this time hunks of black bread and an immense
raw onion.

Out on the hills Pan is not yet dead; if he
sleeps perchance, at least the Nereids are awake.
In the form of lovely women ("fair as a Nereid,"
or "ugly as a Fate," the folk say in their proverbs),
drest in white, with long black hair, they accost
the lonely shepherd or the wayfarer, and woe be to
him if he fails to fend them off. To reply is fatal :
they strike him dumb, or they paralyse a limb, do
him some hurt anyhow. One old man, a storehouse
of ancient lore, told me that as he kept his flocks
by night he heard the Nereids, as it were a great

sound of bells; since when he has heard nothing
plainly, for they made him deaf. If you would
have them harmless, you draw a circle around you
with a black-handled knife, and within this they
cannot come. Nor have the dryads gone, nor the
nymphs of the streams; witness this chapel over
some sacred well, or that tree with its tribute of
rags and onions. All over the land, I might say
in nearly every field, often far from any now in-
habited spot, are ruined shrines or simple enclosures,
each with its patron saint; recalling the corners set
apart for Pan and the nymphs in a Greek farm of
old. Many of these spots have Byzantine remains
upon them, and it is surely not impossible to believe
that some at least may be the very spots where
Pan once was worshipt. They are marked in no
map, and known only in local tradition; and a list
of their saints, if such could be made, might throw
light on their origin. Very many of them are
dedicated to the Virgin, Παναγία, and it is perhaps
not too fanciful to hear in the name an echo of the
old god, when we see how Demeter becomes St
Dimitri, and Eilithyia, St Lephteri (Eleutheros).

The Three Fates still spin their pitiless thread;
on the head of the new-born babe they write his
destiny, and ill luck is for that house where on the
christening night no food is laid for the Sisters.

The evil eye is ever to be guarded against; if it fall upon you, fail not to spit thrice into your bosom, as they did in the days of Theocritus. And when you die, it is Charon who comes grim to fetch you. Hear one of their dirges :—

"Why are the mountain heights so black? why swirl the
    clouds around them?
Is it the hurricane that beats, or rain the hilltops scourging?
It is no hurricane that beats, no rain the hilltops scourging;
'Tis Charos who is passing by with hosts of dead about him.
The young men he drives on before, the greybeards follow
    after,
And all the tender little ones are slung across his saddle."

These dread powers are propitiated much as they used to be. Enter any church of repute: there hang the little votive arms and legs, breasts and faces. There, as in the temple of Asclepius, the night before a great Panegyris, the sick folk sleep in hope of a blessing from the saint. The place looks like a barrack; in the aisles there is no stepping for the beds, rugs, pots and pans, dirty children, and all the paraphernalia of the household; on the carved stalls they sleep two deep. Many are the miracles wrought on them, no less (we may believe) than the wondrous cures of Epidaurus.

But fate, nor Charon, nor dread of disease can make the Greek melancholy. He works as much as he must, to gain food to live on. In winter, if duty takes him out on the hills, he wraps about him a sheepskin thick as a board, and makes the best of it ; when the warm weather comes, he basks in the sunlight, eats his fruit and cheese, drinks his weak wine, and passes most of his time in rolling cigarettes, which consist chiefly of paper. In the evening, he sits at the café and enjoys the latest gossip ; full of animation and vivid talk, laughter, jokes, and stories, hardly ever drinking to excess, and but rarely excited to use the daggers and pistols that stuff his pouch.

Then again, when the holy day comes for the local saint, or be it vintage time and the grapes must be blessed, early in the morning, by sunrise, the whole village will be assembled at the church. Outside the gates donkeys and mules are tethered, hucksters drive a trade ; within the gates, men stand bare-headed, and women veiled, the church full, the yard thronged with the residue ; the priest says his prayers, and an acolyte carries the censer to wave in and out among the crowd ; the offerings of first-fruits are blessed, and baskets of bread and grapes are brought out, each person taking a piece. Till then the pious have eaten none of the grapes in their vineyards. They worship, they go about their day's work, and in the evening down to the sea-shore, where music and dancing make them happy till nightfall, or even (should there be a moon) far into the night. Men and women alike join in the worship; they are not yet educated into unbelief; and their passion for dancing is no whit less strong than their faith. A Greek will always be dancing, even as an Englishman, when he is happy, will sing a comic song.

The charm of these sunny lands, and their people so merry and light-hearted, attracts the thoughts ever to them again. We long to climb the rugged hill paths once more, to see the partridges fly whirring from under our feet, or the eagle sail among the rocks; to lie in the evening beneath the cloudless sky, and hear the innumerable buzzing things that fill the air with life, the moan of the sea on the not distant shores; to feel the whiff of the evening breeze setting off the land; and with all around so untouched by what is ugly in modern life, to dream that the world is three thousand years younger, and that Troy has but just fallen; and half expect to hear Pan piping down there in the glen,

πὰρ ποταμὸν κελάδοντα, παρὰ ῥοδανὸν δονακῆα.

W. H. D. ROUSE.

AFTER MANY YEARS

THE other day I happened to be travelling from our island to the Capital.[1] When I travel, I always like to know who my companions are. On this occasion our steamer had not many passengers aboard; but when we touched at the little town to the north of the island, a man came off whose appearance I thought rather peculiar. He had all the looks and ways of Western Europe; his very walk was of the West; yet he rated his greedy boatman in the purest Romaic. I wondered who on earth he might be.

When the steamer was once more under weigh, I went up to the man, and giving him good-day, opened a conversation.

"May I ask where you come from?" I began.

"That is my home," said he, "the place which, as you see, I am now leaving."

"And whither away, if God will?" I began.

"To Europe. I have spent all my youth in Europe; I just came home for a visit, to see my people, and now I am going back."

[1] Constantinople.

The ice thus broken, we soon became friends. In the evening, as we sat on deck together, gazing upon the quiet sea as it lay before us, and on the mountains opposite, we talked away, each of himself.

It was a long tale he told me, and full of sadness. He begged me never to make it known, except the one small portion which I am about to tell you now.

"I was quite a youngster (so he began) when I first left our island. My journey led me far into strange lands, to far-away Europe, where the light is, so you wise folks say; but full of darkness and mist I found it. Yes, darkness and mist; and its melancholy paths overgrown with the herb of forgetfulness. Twenty years did that deadly herb numb my senses. For twenty years something gnawed at my vitals unseen,—the undying love for home, which not even Europe was strong enough wholly to destroy.

"After these twenty years, this craving overpowered the herb of forgetfulness. Awoke my heart, awoke my mind,—all my being awoke and cried out for home.

"I took ship, and away I sailed—away to these our beloved islands. And there they were still, each in its proper place. There I found them

again, still smiling as they smiled when I turned
my back upon them long ago. And the sun, as
though he knew what sorrows I had had to bear,
thawed me and warmed me until I was numb with
excess of joy.

"The captain of the little boat that was bearing
me home all but shed tears, poor fellow, when he
learnt my history. It was late in the evening when
we arrived; and as our tiny steamer cast anchor
in the bay, all was dark. You could see the
lights kindling one by one in the houses
opposite.

"The old man hurried to his gun to signal our
approach, but it hung fire. Then he ran to the
whistle, and at once began such a din, you might
have thought some dragon had been vomited up
from the bowels of the earth. For half an hour it
shrieked without a pause.

"'Boat ahoy!' cried the look-out man. 'Here
she comes, skipper! They have heard the signal,
and here's the boat coming.'

"The boat ran alongside, with a few handsome
young fellows in her. In a trice all were aboard of
us, and greeting me with their 'Welcome, welcome!'
as shy as could be. Just think of it! Instead of
pelting me with rotten oranges, after all my heart-
lessness, they were actually shy of me, poor fellows!

" ' And who are you ? ' I asked them.

" ' I am your godchild,' says one. ' Your cousin,' says another. ' Your nephew—your brother-in-law.' Ah ! it's a cruel and topsy-turvy world this ; but it has its odd moments of sweetness.

" The boat cut through the waves, and ran up to the landing-place. Scarce was the painter made fast, when off at a run went Uncle Stamátis, to get the credit of being first with the good news.

" ' Now, you can't take me in !' I cried, as I set foot on shore. ' I know you all. There's my uncle—how white he has grown ! There's Zisis, gay old dog ! with that sly laugh of his.'

" For a few minutes I stood still, gathering them all about me. I tried to say something ; I wanted to assure them that nobody was a bit altered, and that they all seemed to me just as if I had never left them. But I could not open my lips. One moment I leaned upon my old uncle's arm ; then we wiped our tears, and moved away from the jetty by light of the lantern.

" As we went, I stopped now and again to look about me. I noticed a new house here, a new road there ; gardens yonder, where I had last seen nothing but a heap of stones ; shops where I could remember the bare rocks. I seemed to have grown twice my former size, so small and shrunken everything seemed to be. I told them this, and they laughed.

" All the way a heavy anxiety tormented me. For a man to meet his mother after so many years was no laughing matter; one must be very brave indeed ; or something might happen to the old dame. So I began to behave very much like a drunken man trying to show that he is not drunk. I walked on stoutly, bringing down my stick upon the ground with a great air of determination. Afterwards the poor old soul herself told me that she had had the same kind of struggle. And then all of a sudden we found ourselves face to face ! In an instant we were locked in each other's arms. We were mute ; not a word was said. Standing by were forty or fifty of our friends and kin, watching with the same feeling of awe as if they saw some holy sacrament. And a sacrament it was to me, the holiest sacrament of my life, when one kiss wiped out the errors of a lifetime.

" I lifted my eyes to look around me, and found myself clasped in the arms of a young woman weeping. They told me it was my sister.

" ' How pretty you are ! ' I said, turning to banter her ; but my words were choked in tears. She was a few months' bride, and beside her stood the husband, awaiting his turn to embrace me. I took his hand, saying, 'It must be you have made her so pretty ! She was a little wild goat when I used to hold her on my knees, a child of four !' Then I turned and looked her in the eyes. 'Now I know you,' I added ; 'bigger, but still the same.'

"And thus with jest and tear I went through that awful joy, the like of which there is none other in the world.

"When we got to the house, they brought me into the sitting-room. The house was very much the same as ever, but the furniture was all changed ; everything now was made in Germany.

"'A curse on thee, Europe !' said I to myself ; 'so we cannot get quit of thee even here !' But before I could utter a word, the house was full of three generations of my family, the two that I knew (all save those who had gone on their last journey), and the new generation which had sprung up after.

"To describe the meeting with each old kinsman or friend would need a longer time than I have to spare. I will only say that each fresh face was a separate riddle, and I guessed the riddles every one, so well remembered were those days long gone by.

"Ah, those bygone days ! Again I felt their delight and their bliss ! There was the cellar with its store of figs, just as it used to be, the cupboard full of sweetmeats, the pancakes of a morning before dawn, all those trifles that mothers contrive to make us children once again, though our hair be gray! The old hearts and the old songs brought back the past again; but when I entered new houses, and looked upon new faces, and heard things that were new, my soul shrank into itself, and I felt a stranger in a strange land. For even here they had brought the rags of 'civilisation' from Syra and the Capital; here too all the old Greek life was 'refined' away, and they had lost their old island customs as they had lost their old songs. Ah, songs of my home that I love so well! I have sung you, I, the sojourner in foreign lands; and these girls that have never been away from home care nothing to remember you any more, but only babble the ditties of the day with their affected and artificial phrasing!

"'Let us go into the country,' said I one day to my mother; 'never mind if it is October. There at least there will be no change.' Neither was there. The old tower, with the poplars near it and the spring hard by, the plane trees further up, the flocks scattered about the hillside, with their bells tinkling in accompaniment to the shepherds' pipes, the sea far below—all, all was the same as ever. These have not grown old, nor ever will. These are still waiting to greet you and to refresh, be you never so weary.

"I led the old dame to the lonely chapel by the sea-shore. We prayed there, we lit a taper, and vowed to pass our last years at home together.

"'Only let me go back once again,' said I, 'and I swear to you I will not be long this time.'

"She saw how I wished it, and she did not say no. Only she turned her eyes to the sea, and sang a snatch of an old song of her husband's, long since dead :

"'The sea has wept and wept her fill ; now on the rocks 'tis beating.
    Again the sea has wept her fill, again on the rocks 'tis beating.'"

KAPETAN GIORGIS

I

THERE is a ghost in many a hamlet, many a hill,
wood, or lonely chapel; indeed, if we look closely,
we find that each single house has some haunting
horror of its own.   Here it is sickness, here death,
there drunkenness, or some other demon poisoning
the air, when all would seem as though comfort
and bliss reigned supreme.

In the island village whither I am about to take
you, the ghost of the place was for many years a
certain Skipper Giorgis.   Now the poor creature
has departed, and made way for some other ghost.

Let us go back some twenty years, and pay a
visit to yon sacred soil.   Let us stand upon the
cape, where once upon a time rose a proud city,
with its navies, with its forts, and its columns of
marble.   And now—how is the mighty fallen!
The ancient acropolis has been degraded to a
Turkish guard-house, a solitary hut; part of the
old city serves for the cemetery; the rest is field
after field strewn with the stones of old ruins.

Often have I gone there after a shower, to gather wild lettuce or snails, and have returned with whole handfuls of broken antiques and potsherds.

The village proper we shall find on its flank, climbing the hillside. Open a window up there, and your heart opens too ; for to the right spreads the sea far as the eye can reach ; in front lies the bay ; and the hills are opposite, dotted with hamlets here and there ; on the left, a plain covered with olive groves, and one stream in the middle— the very plain where once upon a time Orpheus was cast ashore, and hung his lyre upon a willow, and ever since, the nightingales have sung there with a sweetness that has nothing like it ; until a year or two ago, when the Turks cut down the willows, and the river was left bare, and away flew the nightingales after thirty centuries of song.

Now for Kapetan Giorgis. Picture to yourself a middle-aged man of medium height, his features regular, but so sunburnt that you might take him for a Moor. And not his face only, but his whole body was the same, for except rags and tatters, other clothes had he none. Whenever they gave him clothes, down he would sit beside some rock, tearing them up into little shreds, which he pieced together again with string, and wore them so. He never told us why he did that ; but we all knew of it ; and between you and me, I may as well say he was daft.

Kapetan Giorgis used to speak a language all his own ; here and there you might understand a word, but the most of it rattled off his tongue like pebbles falling upon the ground. He seemed altogether serious and wrapt in his thoughts. Even his laugh (and he laughed but seldom) had a strange gravity, as who should say, " All right, Joy my lass, I know thou'rt a trickster, but thou'lt not trick me !"

He never entered the village unless he was hungry. And then, of course, people used to give him something. That den of his was away outside, open to the four winds, towards the old city. There he loved to wander about ; and sooth to say, when I saw him at times amid the ruins he seemed, as it were, the spectre of one of our fore-fathers, risen from the dead to bewail the desolation of his native land.

But who was Kapetan Giorgis ? That I never could learn from the people of the place, and when I asked the man himself, he would turn his face to the sea, mumbling incoherent phrases. Kapetan Giorgis would have remained for ever a mystery, but that one day came one of those long fishing boats, dragging its net into our bay, and I went down to the beach to buy fish.

It was a great event then if one of these long-boats came in ; as great as the mail-steamer's coming nowadays.   And if for nothing else, it is grand simply to see the leaping fish which the fishermen haul up behind them, crying them for sale, and making all the windows rattle with the noise.

I myself (to make full confession) was fond of fish, but far fonder of watching the fishing-boat. Something always drew me towards it.   I used to stand and watch the oars as they beat all together, now rising, now level and still in the air, then plunging again, just as though all the lads that pulled them were worked by a spring.   I watched the circle marked out by the net on the quiet sea, and thought of the tragedy that was taking place down in the depths.   What dreams they must have had yesterday, those luckless fish !   I seemed to see them dart hither and thither in a frenzy, only to find themselves fast caught.   And when I thought that even had they known what a net means,—even had they never stirred from their place, the net would still have got grip of them, I felt an impulse to call out and bid stop the boat, that the fish might have a chance to make their escape.

In half an hour the boat was moored, and the sons of the sea were on the sand in two lines,

hauling in the two cables with short lines wound
about their waists, and springing back, one by one,
to make fast to the cable in a new place their
ropes with the cork at the end, and to join in the
haul once more.   It was a real delight to look at
them.   I have never yet been so fortunate as to
see a picture of this ; yet what a picture it would
make !   Why do not our painters try this subject ?
You would see manly forms, full of grace and
vigour ; muscles you would see that anyone might
envy, breasts of bronze, necks and heads finely
modelled, turned towards the sea, while their
hands tugged and strained at the cable.

Another half hour and the haul was landed.
The fish trembled and flashed upon the net like
stars in the sky.   The lads came thronging around,
and shaking the net over their baskets : red mullet,
barbel, sardines, anchovy, cuttle-fish—all the mani-
fold gifts of the sea.   Down at the bottom was a
fine bream, a five-pounder.   Yannis, the skipper
(who seemed to know me), strung a bulrush
through its gills, and presented it to me with a
smile.   He would take no payment ; so I invited
him to my house to pay him with good wine, and
he promised to come.

II

In the evening Kapetan Yannis put in an
appearance at our house with the gold ring in
his ear, his long fez, and the red kerchief under
his vest. He kicked off his shoes at the entrance,
and came in. He was a man of some fifty years of
age, was Kapetan Yannis, and modest as a maid.
After the usual questions in came the tray; then
—" To you, and happy to see you ! " and down
went his dram. After this he took a few almonds,
which he cracked with his teeth ; and as his
knotty fingers picked out the kernels, he began
to amuse us with his talk.

Two or three more drams of mastick and we sat
down to our meal. Kapetan Yannis ate like a
man, one end of his napkin tucked into his collar.
And like the stout seaman that he was, with still
greater gusto he drank his wine. When we arose
from the table his eyes were sparkling; all that
first shyness had passed off, and he entertained us
with a flow of tales and quaint pleasantries.

One thing led to another, and, by-and-bye, mention was made of Kapetan Giorgis. At this name
our guest looked confused. Seeing that he must
know something about our spectre, I tried to draw
him out. At first he would not open his lips ;

but when the women had retired, after much
pressing and vows never to tell a soul, he began
the following story :

"He and I come from the same place," said he,
after pulling out a handkerchief and mopping his
face—"from the same place, and I am his brother-
in-law. He was a fisherman's son, but he had a
great deal in him, and he was determined to rise
in the world. And then he had his eye on a girl
who was very well off; and she loved him, too, for
he was a fine young fellow, that he was. But
before he could propose for the girl he ought to
dower and wed his three sisters, and then make a
position for himself too. Well, they agreed between them to wait a few years, and then he was
to send the match-makers.

"And so out goes Giorgis into the world; and,
working with all his heart, in one year he managed
to get a boat of his own. In another year the
boat became a smack. And every year back came
the skipper from his voyages, in high spirits, and,
look you, each year he married off one sister.
What jollifications there were at those weddings !
if there was one blessing for the bride and bridegroom there were two for him, since each wedding
brought him a step nearer to his sweetheart. At
the third wedding I was the bridegroom, and it's

enough to say that the rascals kept me away from my bride a whole day and night with their merry-makings.

"The poor fellow tried to make his own match that time; and would to God he had made it! The dowers had swallowed up all he had, sure enough, but people knew him now for a clever fellow, and that was worth a great deal for Giorgis. But then, you see, even the smack was mortgaged with building house after house for his sisters. At last we told him, a proud man is the girl's father—go one voyage more, and next year come and woo thy beauty.

"I well remember the evening when he took the musicians and went serenading beneath her windows, and sang to her as he went by, without stopping, for fear her people might smell a rat (they knew nothing about it)—

"'Now fare thee well, my golden dove, I soon shall be departed;
  Forth from the window peep above, that I may go light-hearted.'

And a window half opened in the upper storey.

"Next day the smack got under weigh, and Kapitan Giorgis was firing farewell salutes to his lady-love.

"Eleven months went by, and we had heard

nothing. In the twelfth month a terrible rumour
buzzed among us. The lady was said to be
betrothed to some rich stranger, who was for
marrying with her in hot haste, to carry her off
forthwith. And true it was, too. The whole
thing was begun and done in a twinkling. The
girl protested, wept, besought, threatened; all in
vain. She was hugged off to the priest, and before
the week was out the stranger had carried her off
to his home, dowry and all, to poison our life without blessing his own; for the poor lass fell into a
consumption, and in a few months all was over.

"The wedding party left one day in the morning, and next evening late brought the caïque with
Giorgis into our bay. It was a peaceful evening,
and once again his gun spoke out, and waked the
echoes among the hills. No one came down to the
landing-place but myself, for I knew him well, and
feared that the rest might drive him mad somehow.
Little did I think what was coming!"

Again Kapetan Yannis pulled out his handkerchief to mop his face.

"Ah, sir, that was an awful evening! The
sailors had begun to furl the sails, Giorgis went
shooting away and singing all the time, and I must
stand all alone upon the landing-stage, and my
heart ready to burst! The caïque remained out-

side the harbour till the entrance should be free from some fishing boats that just then were passing through, so George came ashore in the dinghy, and soon he was before me. When he saw me standing pensive and half stupefied, says he—

" ' Hullo, Yannis, what's up ? Anybody dead ? Tell me, and have done with it.'

" As I tried, faltering, to say that there had been no death, he brought me up sharp with— ' Well, what is it then ? Married ? '

" I could hold out no longer, but began to sob. He stared hard at me, and turned as yellow as sulphur, but not a word, only gnawed his moustache in a mad sort of way, then suddenly into the boat, and off.

" I lost my head, for I should have jumped in with him. I called after him, and adjured him by his father's soul, but he would not hear. By the time I could find another boat to carry me aboard him, he was at the helm of his caïque, which now turned seawards again. In a little while she had disappeared over the sea.

" All this I saw with my own eyes, the rest I will tell in a few words, for time flies, and the lads will overdo it down at the inn. I will tell the story just as I heard it a few days later from the crew.

" Kapetan Giorgis let his vessel run before the wind, and the north wind carried her straight on what you call the Broad Beach. 'Twas night, and about a league off the land the skipper called his men, and ordered them to get in the boat and go where they would. The men looked at each other in dismay, and hesitated, but the skipper, seizing the gun, showed them he was in grim earnest. The end of it was, they took the boat and headed her for the beach, but they still kept an eye behind, for it seemed as if something was wrong with the skipper. A little while and they saw the caïque running full sail upon a headland some half a mile beyond the cape. In a trice the boat's head was round, and straight for the rock, but when they got there the caïque had disappeared, and he with her. As soon as ever he came to the surface, half dead, one of them gript him, pulled him into the boat, and got him ashore. His breath came back to him by-and-bye, but neither wit nor speech ever again returned.

" There, master, you have the whole story," added Kapetan Yannis, with tears in his eyes.

" One thing more." I said, " how was it you didn't take him back home again ? "

" Couldn't be done. He must have lost his wits before ever he sank the vessel. When they had

saved him and got him ashore, they found him a
hopeless imbecile. They tried to keep him in a
house till one of us could go over, but he would
not stir from the spot. When I came I found him
stretched on the shingle by the sea-shore, and proposed that we should go home,—'twas all one as if I
spoke to a stone. Gradually he found voice to
mutter as he does now, and from his half words I
soon perceived that the mischief was past curing.
One day I got him aboard a caïque by force, and
he jumped like a cat and swam away. Now I pay
him a visit twice in the year. I find him down
yonder among the tombs of the Turkish cemetery;
for mad though he be, he is sane enough to wish
no one to know that I am anything to him. He
wants to remain unknown here. I take his clothes,
and he first tears them to rags and then wears them.
He's a living shipwreck himself, poor soul, with his
mind stopt short for ever, gone to the bottom as
sure as that ship that sank with all he had in the
world."

Yannis' lips were trembling as he spoke.

"A glass of wine, Kapetan," said I, "to drive
dull care away! Ah, what a sad world this
is!"

"To you, sir, and may we soon meet again!"
And he tossed off the parting glass with a

dogged air, as though struggling to drown his troubles.

Next day, as the long-boat was sailing away, I saw Kapetan Giorgis tearing up a new cape, muttering the while and gazing upon the sea.

PAPPA SOPHRONIOS

It was the month of August. The grapes were ripe, the figs sweet as honey, and the olives had begun to turn yellow away up on the topmost twigs. Scent of thyme and marjoram was wafted over the hills, and made it a pure delight to breathe.

In that country, the most delightful part of the day was not the dawn, when the hills smiled as the sun looked upon them; not midday, when the cicala dinned us deaf; not the evening hour, when we came down to the strand, and watched the fish that leapt flashing into the air, as though the sea could not hold them. No; but there the sweetest of all was night, to sit in the garden around the tower, under the cherry trees by the side of the spring, the ever-babbling spring; where the croaking frogs, the bells of the flocks ringing and ringing around, the whispering ripple of sea on shore, made the sweetest music that ever was heard by man. And I had almost forgotten the choicest note of all—the chirp of grasshoppers in the

22

grass, incessant as the cicala, but not so bold : a modest melody, tender, peaceful as those serene nights.

Yet a little, and the breeze would begin to blow back off the land,—"the valley drew it down," as we used to say ; and bathed us in a delicious cool, enough to make an old man young. The first to announce this change in the wind were the poplars about the spring, with an angry and deep roar.

There we were used to spend our evenings in summer-time. There we listened to many a story, many a song. There our old men would tell their reminiscences, vying one with another who should give us the oldest tales and the prettiest. And when the old men were weary, lads and lasses began their songs and their music.

Then came the "gray man" (our name for sleep), and took us captive one after one.

Not far from that unforgotten garden was a little vineyard with a hut in one corner of it. Within that hut, all by himself, sat an old priest, smoking his chibouk ; and this was Pappa Sophronios.

The old Pappa—God forgive me for saying it— was not exactly a handsome man ; and full of all sorts of oddities he was. "Father Loony" they

called him up in the village. Beaked like a bird,
a beard like a goat's beard, white at the ends, and
round the mouth yellow with constant smoking, a
face all wrinkled and browned, eyes that sparkled,—
perhaps from drinking much wine—and there you
have Pappa Sophronios.

When he performed the service in his church, he
used to terrify us with his cracked voice. When
he read the prayers, you might suppose him to be
shouting orders to the labourers in his vineyard.
He was always fussing about that little estate of
his. Perhaps his being so fond of that bit of a
farm was no great sin in the worthy Father. It is
a venial fault, not uncommon among our priests,
and indeed, more to be imitated than blamed. It
was priest's hat in the village, peasant's cap and
pruning knife in the fields. After all, *orare est
laborare;* and this is a sermon better a thousand
times than the high-flown discourses we often hear
from a popular pulpit.

Pappa Sophronios was unlettered, eccentric, and
cracked; he cared not twopence for the world.
Now he would go on the spree with some of his
lay friends; then again, St Anthony himself was not
so holy a saint. When the whim took him, he made
a mock of anybody, and trusted no one. What game
I made of him, when some old widow woman, not

remarkable for her faithfulness while her husband lived, begged him to pray for the dead man's soul in the service, and he pulled a malicious grin behind her back, as who should say—"So you have learnt wisdom too! Well, better late than never!"

Well, as we sat one evening in the garden by the watch-tower, all half-asleep, said one of us:

"Let us call Pappa Sophronios to come and wake us up. One pull of wine, and he'll soon begin to talk!"

No sooner said than done; and we had him cross-legged on the stone seat which ran along the wall of the tower, with his chibouk, and the wine by his side. He always loved to discourse on things which no one living had seen but himself, and perhaps one or two more; but on that evening not a word could be got out of him. He seemed to be wrapt up in his own thoughts.

"What's up, Pappa," said some one, "that you won't talk to us this evening? The crops promise well."

"Ah well, my children, I am sadder and wiser than I was yesterday. Poor Aunt[1] Daphnoula is gone! I buried her myself. I tried in vain to

---

[1] "Aunt" does not imply kinship, but is a kind of pet title for old women. "Uncle" is used in the same way of men.

see on her face the smile of her younger days, as I
remember it in my mind!"

This sounded odd to us who knew the old dame.
Aunt Daphnoula was the widow of Uncle Lephtéris,
the man who was crushed in an earthquake because
he was too drunk to get away; he left her a widow
at sixty; she used to carry the water herself to her
melon plot, and sometimes brought us the first
ripe fruit, for which we would give her bread, or
maybe something to wear.   What could we do but
burst out laughing, to hear Pappa Sophronios moral-
ising in this way about the old woman who had
gone that morning to her account?

"Ah, my children, you laugh; but if you knew,
if you only knew!"   And he cast a glance towards
Aunt Daphnoula's little field.

Unable to guess what was the matter, we
looked significantly at one another.   Then I
noticed that his eyes were actually full of tears;
and thinking this must be some real trouble, I
said to him:

"Tell us all about it, Father, whatever it is that
is making you unhappy.   Hitherto we have confessed to your reverence; now you shall confess to
us.   We are friends and neighbours; no one is
here but ourselves, and God."

He turned to us with a somewhat happier

look ; and without more ado proceeded to relate his story.

"Yes, I will tell you, my children ; I should like to tell it to you now, when she is gone, and ere long I shall have gone to follow her. I have no friends but you. Serra is my home, where my people lived. What has become of them, God knows. Fifty years ago !

"When I tumbled head over heels into this village, a lad of twenty, Uncle Yannis took me into his shop down there at the Landing ; he married Reginouda, you know, the sister of Hadji [1] Gligóris, whom the Turks beheaded for building our church one foot higher than the firman allowed. Uncle Yannis had a fine portion with the girl ; but it soon went, till nothing was left but that little plot of Aunt Daphnoula's.

"Well, at that time, says Uncle Yannis to me, 'Sotíris'—that was my name—'you are no good for the shop ; go and work in the fields.' As for me, what else did I want ? We had always been tillers of the soil, the whole lot of us, from father to son.—In six months I had made the little plot a garden. You remember that old stump down by the spring ? It used to

---

[1] "Pilgrim" i.e., one who has been to Jerusalem.

be the finest of all the olive trees over there.
Now it's a dead stump, like me.

"Away behind the hill, down by the seaside,
there used then to be our old shrine of the Saints
Unfeed;[1] but at that time it was only a circuit of
stones, with an oleaster beside it hung all over with
rags, which mothers used to put there to cure their
children's diseases ; and the holy table was a stone
too.   Now the shrine is gone with the rest, for they
have built it in.   Now you enter a dark hut when
you want to worship.

"It was the thirtieth of the Harvest,[2] the vigil of
St Cosmas and St Damian.   People gathered from
far and near to the feast.   The feast is held still, but
most people don't start till the morning, when they
come and pay their worship, some of them going back
at once, some staying the day out to return when
evening falls.   In those days, every one used to be
there overnight ; and the gathering for the feast
took place on the eve of it, and they kept it up all
night long.   What a to-do there was, what com-
motion !   Every field had a bonfire in the middle,
there was a swing in every tree.   The lads made
merry around the fires, the girls sat on the swings
and sang.   You could hardly hear the songs, so soft
and quiet they used to sing them in those days.

[1] St Cosmas and St Damian, who cured the sick without fee.
[2] June.

"Over yonder, my children, below the great olive tree, which now is a bare stump, there sat Sotíris and listened to Daphnoula, Uncle Yannis' lass, as she sang from her swing in the tree :

"'Trembles the fish at fisher's sight, the lamb to see the slayer ;
Trembles my heart at yon brave lad, whose coming doth affray her.'

"As for a poor devil like me—I built my castles in the air, and took the words in all earnestness, not thinking what a fright I was to look at, and their servant too ; and how young Lephtéris, who had just returned from Anatolia, and had both money and good looks,—how he was the man that Daphnoula had in mind, and her mother too. Women don't look at the heart, my children ; money and fine looks is all they think of, and that was the reason why they failed to understand me that evening. But I didn't know the world then, and I was duped. No one ever had the laugh of me again ; but that time I was fairly duped.

"But why make a long story of it ? A few days, and they were betrothed ; and when Easter time had passed, there was Daphnoula a bride, for all the village to admire, going to church with her flutters and her downcast eyes, the music in front, and the priests not far away. A week long the festivities lasted. In those days weddings were not as they are now, done in a twinkling, 'light and dout,' as they say. They lasted a whole week then, and a big feast every day. It's too long to tell you all about it; there was the day they brought the bride to the bath, the day they boiled the wheat-broth, then the day that the trunks were brought over, next day they sent the milk-cakes round, and the broidered kerchiefs, the next day they drest the bride, and all the girls of the place gathered round her to sing those endless songs of theirs. And the nights again; a perfect pandemonium it was, what with the drink and the singing. Every one, man and woman, must dance then, the old dames with the rest. And it was something more than lute and viol; first old Trakos used to sing, his fiddle fastened about his waist, then it was up with his bow, and fire away! How many boards they broke, and how many glasses! Night after night they went on drinking, the beggars! But then it was only wine, and hurt nobody.

"There now—I have gone and forgotten all about my story. Forgive me, my children!——Well, it was Monday morning, and we had taken the bridegroom out to Cool Springs for the washing. This took place, as it does now, the day after the crowning of the pair. So at daybreak we all turned out to go and give the bridegroom his bath. I went out with the rest, feeling most miserable, and poured the water over his hands that he might go fresh to his Daphnoula. My hand trembled as I poured; I knew not what I was doing, or what I was thinking. And now I will confess to you, my children, in God's holy presence, what I did in that moment, that afterwards you may pray God to pardon mine offence. I cursed him at that moment and prayed in my heart, 'As this water is poured out and flows away, so may all his joys flow away from him.' The curse took him, curse it! It took him, and within two years he fell into drunken ways, and made ducks and drakes of all the bride's dower. Only that little plot yonder was left, and was useful to Daphnoula, poor thing, after her man was killed by the drink.

"After the wedding I was well-nigh bereft of my wits. Day and night I wandered about the hills up yonder, and tried to work off my feelings with groans and love-ditties. That must have been how I cracked my voice.

"When Lephtéris had got his wife's property into his own hands, and had settled down a little after the wedding festivities, the first thing he did was to get rid of me. He must have scented something or other. Something I must have blurted out in my sleep, which got to his ears. Perhaps it was God's will; for I went straight to the Cathedral and took holy orders, and came into your parish to stay for the rest of my life.

"Fifty years have gone by since then. Daphnoula had a thousand poisons to drink; then she was left a widow, childless and with no means of subsistence but her little plot of land; and never in all those years has she heard one word from my lips, except 'God's blessing on thee' when I gave her the Communion bread of a Sunday or Holy Day. As I looked upon her, I called myself the murderer of her Lephtéris. It was the curse, that curse that gnawed within me; I did my best towards it with my prayers, but it was too late.

"You know now, my children, why I have been an eccentric kind of priest, and why sometimes I kicked over the traces, both in my young days and later. I was not the same as a lad; life and trouble have made me what I am. How often have I said in my sinful heart, 'Why does God look from above upon all this, and does not stretch forth his holy hand to save us, before the devil catches us with his hook?'

"But it grows late, my children. Receive my blessing, sinner though I be. Give me yours, though you are but children. Good-night to you! You are the only ones who know this; not even your departed grandfather knew it, God rest his soul! I have seen much and suffered much. Good-night."

.   .   .   .   .

In a few moments we heard nothing but the spring, the frogs, the grasshoppers, the ripple of the waves. It seemed to us like a dream that had come and gone. We awoke again from those years of long ago, whose story the old men were never tired of telling; but we awoke pensive and sad. And next morning we awoke from sleep to hear that Pappa Sophronios had been found dead upon his pallet of straw.

BLIND KOSTAS' WIFE

Who would ever expect that after a shower would sprout up a story! Yet such miracles do happen. Had there been no shower up on Mount St Elias, had not the cataracts of heaven burst upon that lofty peak, and if I had not been guided to a certain village to spend the night, I should not now be able to tell you the story of Blind Kostas' wife.

I was returning from town; one day's journey, with hills and stones as many as you will: but I had a good guide who knew how to speak to his mule, and a mule which knew how to obey. The poor beast climbed the footpaths amidst thorns and brambles like a goat, and with a movement so gentle that he did not fatigue you. All that irked me was the pack-saddle, with a rope or two at the side holding my luggage.

It was half an hour after sunset, and we wanted three hours more to get home. But the moon was half full, and we reckoned to climb the hill and get down into our plain by its light. Hardly had we said as much, when the clouds began to gather.

We happened to be then in a little wood. One sudden flash, and the ball began. The thunder deafened us ; the bolt must have struck close by, we thought, and said so ; before the words were out of our lips another bombardment greeted us amid the wilderness. Again there were a few moments of silence, and then a deep, incessant uproar began. It was the great drops beating upon the leaves. The storm grew worse moment by moment, until it became a veritable deluge. Now and again it lightened and thundered, and from flash to crash took no longer time than I take to tell it. There was a regular hurricane on that hill.

When we got out of the wood, we were drenched to the skin, and our clothes were clinging about us. The storm now began to abate, and soon ceased entirely ; the black clouds passed, and the moon smiled out again. But I did not feel like smiling just then, for I was shivering ; it was October, too. So I said to the man : " Suppose we take refuge in that village, down on the slope yonder."

In half an hour my mule's hoofs were striking sparks on the stones in the lane which divided the village into two halves. A coffee-house and two or three little shops, with half-a-dozen sunburnt villagers sitting outside, showed me that we had reached the market-place.

We enquired at the coffee-house where we could find a night's lodging.

" You are welcome," said a man.

I thought this man was willing to entertain us, so leaping off my mule, I returned his salute, and asked him the way to his house. But I speedily found that his " welcome " was a mere greeting ; for so the village folk use, with a " welcome " and a " good-day " for every stranger, even if they have never set eyes on him before. True good breeding sheds its fragrance among these hills.

So I asked again where we could have shelter for the night.

" Why, at Mrs Blindeyes, to be sure !" says the good fellow.

I had been thinking, as I passed through the village, that I might chance upon some wild flower born to blush unseen, and on hearing this, I said to myself : " Mrs Blindeyes ! There's my wild flower !"

So a boy came with us, bearing a lantern to show us the way to the house of Mrs Blindeyes.

It seemed as though they must have got wind of coming guests, for awaiting us at the gate stood a lad of sixteen or so, candle in hand, and with him a man got up bravely in a fez just off the block, short jacket and vest of woollen stuff, woollen breeches, hanging evenly and without folds ; a wide girdle, neatly folded; white stockings, and slippers turned down at the heel, and holding a small string of beads in his hand.[1] This last was the village schoolmaster, called (it would appear) to do the honours of the place.

A vine was trained so as to cover the courtyard, and fallen leaves showed that here, too, a heavy storm must have passed. The lad led off my man to show him the way to the stable and the kitchen; and me the schoolmaster led into the house. There was an inner yard that shone for cleanliness, a stair made of planks yellow as amber, leading up to a kind of balcony or *loggia*, with a long lounge on one side of it; opposite to us was the door of the best room; in the other wall was a door which opened into the " Inner House," the house proper, a sort of holy of holies, about which it may not be out of place to say something, as these are gradually becoming a thing of the past. They have not built one these fifty years.

The " Inner House " is always built on the same plan. The walls are thick as the walls of a castle, and built of large stones, running the whole length of the house and half its breadth. The room is divided into two parts: one, the lower part, taking

---

[1] This is no rosary ; but the Levantine Greeks and Turks usually carry such a string, with which their fingers perpetually fidget.

up two-thirds of the whole space; and the other,
being a kind of daïs, standing some two or three
feet above the floor, with a pair of steps in the
middle to mount by.   Under this daïs is the fig-
cellar, which you find full of huge earthen jars, and
these, again, full of dried figs, almonds, nuts, con-
serves, olives black and olives white, whole olives
and broken olives.   The daïs is surrounded by long
couches.   In this part are the windows, which look
out into the garden.   Sometimes a jasmine climbs
and twines about the window lattice.

In the lower portion of this " Inner House," besides the shrine for the icon[1] (where must be
placed all the patron saints of the village and of
the family), all the household treasures are hung
on the walls and put on the shelves by way of
ornament: large, round trays; dishes; pots and
pans, all of copper, all burnished and brightened;
then there are the plates and the glasses, and, last
of all (if they have nothing else), they arrange rows
of quinces, pomegranates, melons, and other kinds
of fruit.   But the finest of the fruit you will see
hanging in nets from the roof, which is black, and
sometimes (with the roof-tree) tricked out in patterns
of red.   The roof outside is flat, and covered with a
layer of seaweed and soil on the top; after a shower

[1] A sacred picture of some saint.

the soil is always rolled with a stone roller, to keep it flat and to prevent the dripping of the water.

The floor of this room is spread with carpets in the winter time. Here, instead of long couches, we have low soft seats, a kind of mattress in fact; and for seats, the wall is lined with chests containing the family heirlooms and the bride's dower hidden within them. The fireplace in the corner no one ever kindles nowadays; all we have now is a chafing dish. But in times gone by, fires burned bright in the fireplace, and the family used to stretch themselves out and sleep in front of the burning logs. Now it has become an ornament, and white as snow from the everlasting daub, daub, daub with whitewash. Over the fireplace are shelves one above another, holding the best china, and at the end of the lowest shelf a censer for the family shrine. There is no light but what comes from the lamp hanging in the fireplace, and the taper lit in front of the icons.

This will give you a fair idea of the place. And now, I would ask you, the young generation of our ancient race, who spend your last farthing in travelling to Europe, why not make a trip each year amongst our islands, to see all these things, and much else that is even more strange and beautiful,—to learn about them, to love them, these things which are your very own, all without dipping deep into your purse ? Why do you only care to hurry to foreign parts, never perceiving that even in this Europe of yours the greatest peoples are those which prize what is their own, those national customs which you hold so cheap; and that one day the Franks themselves will come flocking thither, to lounge about and observe that the old-world grace and beauty of the Odyssey has life in it still ! When that happens we shall love these old things too, not from our own taste but because it is the fashion. Go, go, I beg you, and visit one fresh island every year. You will find hospitality and friends, pleasures you will find that no money could buy in Europe ; and you will return to your dusty Athens with heart open and lungs refreshed.

After I had changed my things in a handsome bedroom, and the maid had poured water over my hands, which I wiped dry on the towel she gave me, I passed into the "Inner House," and saw before me a lady who welcomed me in a quiet and sweet voice, and with a smile half repressed. I had expected to see some old hag with one eye at the most ; and now, here was this beautiful lady, with two eyes, big and black, that had in them still all the fire and all the brilliancy of youth ! She wore a little fez, and twined about it was a kerchief

covered with gold coins, with a blue silk tassel
spread over the top ; she had on a pearl necklace,
from which over her bosom hung a Byzantine gold
coin. The wide trousers which she wore could not
be seen then, for in those days women used a flow-
ing skirt. Dame Despina[1] (this name suited her
better than Mrs Blindeyes) had also a dark petticoat,
and over her shoulders a fine light pelisse of fur.

Farther in, upon the low soft couch, was a bene-
volent-looking man, handsome like his wife. He
half rose, and gave us welcome with a strange sort
of smile. This was Blindeyes Kostas, the husband
of the angelic Despina. Blindeyes they called him,
because sight the poor fellow had none.

Our talk, when we found ourselves seated, was
simple and unrestrained. I told them who I was,
and they recognised my name. It was embarrassing
not to know anything of them, seeing that I had to
do with the most distinguished family in the village ;
a family humble once, and plunged in poverty, but
now first in fortune and in good name. In a few
minutes entered their son, a bright lad with flashing
eyes. "A son of true love !" said I to myself,
when I recognised him again ; he it was who had
held the light for us in the gate.

After a chat of some half-hour or so, the table

[1] The word itself means "Lady."

was laid. The maid entered and took down the
largest tray from the wall; this she placed upon a
stand inlaid with mother-of-pearl; all around she
arranged pillows, and laid on each one of those long
embroidered napkins which they all put over their
knees when sitting down to meat; when this was
all ready, the food was brought in. Dame Despina,
who had been absent a few moments to see how
things were going on in the kitchen, now returned
and invited us to fall to. Then leading her husband by the hand, she placed him by her own side.

We made the sign of the cross for a blessing,
said our set phrase of thanks, and began. Our
host (we had a light on the table by this time, and
I could see better) was a man full of life. Every
bit of him seemed to talk, all but his eyes; they
alone had nothing to say. He was eager to hear
all I had heard and seen during my travels; and
while I told him, forgot his meal, and as though he
were striving with all his might to see me, he sat,
spoon in hand, his lips playing and trembling with
satisfaction and curiosity.

The lady of the house had not much to say, but
that little well-weighed and put in words carefully
chosen. She had but to give a glance, to utter
one sentence, in order to win respect. There was
a dainty grace in her face, her mouth, her neck,

her small hands, in every feature and every movement; and above this grace sat power enthroned, a
character which you might think God had formed
to show how much blessedness could be sent down
into this world of ours.

The lad said nothing, unless in answer to some
question; he ate with excellent appetite, and cared
not at all how they teased him for it. The schoolmaster, too, did his duty, both at cup and trencher.
He showed no less curiosity in hearing my adven-
tures; and if I happened to mention some place
which they did not know, he was kind enough to
explain the geography for their benefit—a little,
perhaps, as if he held pointer in hand, yet without
over much of the pedagogue in his manner. He
too had seen the world; had he not been as far as
Athens?

The meal done, the maid brought in a basin and
we washed our hands; then the table was removed,
and Dame Despina fetched her needlework; but
we still went on talking. The lad's eyes were
rivetted on my face; never before, his mother said,
had he been known to keep awake after supper.
So passed another half-hour, when I asked them
to excuse me, as I was tired, and bade them good-
night; and the school-master returned home.

As I stretched my limbs on the soft and welcome

bed, I cast about how I could learn the history of
Mrs Blindeyes. A history there must surely be,
between such a wife and such a husband. I thought
of this and I thought of that, and at last I hit upon
a plan. It was Saturday evening; there was no
school next day: well, I would take the schoolmaster in my company, and he should tell me the
story. And so it happened.

 .   .   .   .   .

When I got up in the morning, after the usual
spoonful of preserved fruit and cup of coffee, I
bade a friendly farewell to my hosts, begging them
some day to return my visit; then mounting my
mule, I rode along the market - place. I had
intended to seek out the school, and so find the
schoolmaster; but he happened to be in the coffee-
house drinking his morning cup after service. I
asked him for the pleasure of his company on my
journey home, where he could spend the night and
return on Monday morning. Experienced traveller
though he was, he thought the journey too long;
however, after much talking, I persuaded him to
come with me half-way, so as to return at midday;
and the end of it was he saddled a stout ass and
we set out.

That journey was undiluted pleasure, as we
jogged along through the olive groves; and the

pleasantest part of it was to see the lads beating
the trees, and the maids gathering the fruit beneath. It was Sunday, true, but then they had
no time to lose, now that winter had come so swift
upon them.

Through scenes like these we proceeded, with
many a question as to this property and that;
until we came opposite to the gardens and orchards
of Mrs Blindeyes.

" A large property," said I to the schoolmaster.
" They must be rich people."

" Well, they were poor enough once," was his
reply.

" Anyhow, there's money made here, you can
see that. Now tell me, there's a good fellow—
how did they get it? And how came that fine
old fellow blind? and who is that charming wife of
his? Tell me all about her. We have an hour or
so before us yet."

" God sent His blessing upon their doings,
and——"

" Now look here, my dear master; it's Sunday
to-day, I know, but I ask you to do me a favour.
Leave that Sunday tongue of yours behind in the
village, and keep to the one you use on week-days.
How do you suppose your donkey is going to carry
the other as well, with all its tricks and trappings?

Throw it away, my dear fellow, and think of your young days; tell me the whole story as your mother, God bless her, told it to you!"

The schoolmaster was a man of sense, and took me in a trice. He gave a hearty laugh, thought for a few moments, and then began:

"I must carry you back some eighteen years or so, when Dame Despina was a girl of twenty, and so beautiful that all the young fellows in the place sang songs in her praise. She was an orphan, and lived then in the same house where she lives now. She had a little piece of land besides, that little corner behind the plane tree yonder. She had nothing else belonging to her but an aunt, old Aunt Permathoula, the mourning woman, who used to crack the very stones with her lamenting as she followed the corpse—

> 'Wae's the woof, and wae's the weft,
> Wae to me, what hae I left!'

—'Woe to me, what have I left,' she meant.

"Good luck to you, my dear schoolmaster; God bless you! Can't you see that the words are precisely the same?"

The schoolmaster smiled and went on.

"Dame Despina was poor; but two precious jewels she had,—beauty and honour. Rare, indeed, it is, in that wide world in which you wander, to find these two jewels together. Here in the high-lands we often find those two flowers growing side by side."

I did not care to contradict him, for fear of losing the story, so I let him run on.

"She was sitting one evening, a Saturday even-ing it was, on the lounge in the Inner House, with her embroidery before her. She was betrothed to Kostákis, I must tell you, Lampros' son, and all the village was delighted with the lovers. All day long she sang over her embroidery, and all day Kostas sang over his work in the fields; a fine young fellow he was, and a voice like honey. Well, as I was saying, when the sun set on that Saturday evening, up rose the girl, lit a candle, and swung the incense; then she made herself tidy, and went to the window to water her flowers. Just then came the sound of a voice, her aunt, the mourning woman, from the courtyard—

"'Avaunt! avaunt! to the hills, to the moun-tains, to the twigs, to the barren trees!¹ What is this great evil that has come upon us?'

"It was to Aunt Kantaxiné that these words were addressed, when she came and told her the black news. And what news it was! Poor Kostas had fired a mine in some piece of ground where

¹ A charm commonly used in Lesbos.

they were blasting, and before he could get out of the way the powder caught ; it had singed all his face, and blinded him in both eyes. They carried him home half dead. They laid him upon a couch, and awaited the doctor who had been summoned from another village ; all the wailing women of the neighbourhood flocked in, and when they saw his mother tearing her hair, and Kostas groaning in his pain, such a lamentation they made that it was worse than a death. I was there too, a boy of twelve, and saw it with my own eyes. And that was nothing ; worse followed when that lovely maiden came, along with her aunt, pallid as pale gold, her two great eyes open wide with terror, speechless, and never a tear! What tears fall in such hours as that? The tears come afterwards, when the storm has past and the heart has grown soft.

" I mind how the wretched Kostas perceived that she was beside him, and how he tried to comfort her, saying there was nothing the matter, and he would soon be well. His voice could not be heard for a long time, as Aunt Permathoula, the mourner, had burst out into a lament that terrified the whole neighbourhood, and the other old women too, they sobbed and sobbed with their aprons over their eyes.

" Amidst all this misery the only one who bore

up was the girl. She rose like a queen among them, and bade them hold their peace. And then the strength of this rare woman was shown. All fell silent; they prepared the bed, and laid the young man in it. And now all the mourners were changed into nurses. One of them brought rose-cakes, another mallows, a third miraculous icons to save his life. About midnight the doctor came, and as soon as he saw Kostas, told us that for the eyes there was no cure.

"Forty days and forty nights the unhappy Despina sat by her lover's side. They told her it was not modest for a betrothed maid to sit like that, day in day out, by the side of a young man. ' He is my husband ! ' she said, turning upon them. ' No one has a right to call me to account. I will nurse him until he is well, and then I will marry him.' And her voice choked in sobs.

"People took these for the ravings of sorrow. However, when Kostas rose from his sick bed, she took him one morning by the hand and led him to her house, dressed in her best, and along with the aunt—who had no word in the matter, willy nilly —went to church, all three of them. How people rubbed their eyes then, to be sure, and said, ' Poor girl, what a sad thing for her ! '

" ' A sad thing for you that think so,' said she,

stretching out her beautiful hand in its sleeve covered with fine lace.

" Much to her joy the priest made no difficulty about marrying them ; he knew that she had a good dowry from her mother. So in an hour's time Kostas was quit of all his troubles, except that he could not see the treasure which God had given him. Nay, the poor fellow even made merry at his misfortune, saying that blindness had brought him one blessing at least, in marrying him all the sooner.

" Love—the true love that turns everything into milk and honey—at once began to reign in their home. It was August, and without delay Despina set hard to work. She had large plans in her mind ; she was ambitious and proud, and deter- mined to show the world that pitied her what a blind man's wife can do.

" All day long she worked on her land, while Kostas carried water to the olives and the figs, feel- ing his way along the walls. Or sometimes he would take the lute, and sing to his beauty as she worked.

" In this way some two years passed by. Their baby was born, and people began to wonder at the marvellous luck that attended the house of the blind man. So much so, that many a maid broke her jest upon it, vowing that she would herself look out for a blind husband. Whatever the woman touched turned to gold. Their fruit was the finest, and people were willing to pay extra if they could buy from blind Kosta's fields. Fields, I say, because there were three of them by this time, and afterwards they became as many as you have seen.

"Two or three years went by, and Despina now no longer need labour with her own hands. She had her man-servants and her maid-servants. She was a lady now, and the part suited her. No one grudged it to her, for her heart was ever the same. All respected her, and they feared her too, for her word was weight and strength. It came to this, that she was asked to be arbiter in other people's disputes, such a man's head was upon those fair shoulders.

"As for Kostas, he did not wish to be idle, so he joined the church choir. But now he has given up his music; his delight now is to hear his boy Petros read aloud of an evening. During the day he passes his time partly with the neighbours, partly amid his round of trifles. His lady finds no time to sit still, though Petros looks after the fields. What with housekeeping and what with her neighbours' troubles, she is always busy. Every nest of poverty and distress she manages to ferret out.

She has her help for this one, money for that, gifts
in kind for the other; it is her joy to do good.   If
a stranger comes into our village, it is to the Mrs
Blindeyes' house he must go.   That's what happened to you, sir."

"And a good thing it was for me," said I to the
schoolmaster; "I only wish I had known last night
that my entertainer was so true a queen.   God
knows when I shall pass by your village again !"

Here we parted, the schoolmaster turning his
face homewards, and I making my way down to
our plain, which now began to be visible in the
distance.

MARINOS KONTARAS

From my boyhood I have been fond of my little
pleasure trips. I used to take nets and tackle
aboard some boat, and fish or not as I felt inclined.
If I did not care to fish, and there was a bit of a
breeze, then it was up yard and out sail, and away
I sped over the sea, till chance brought me to some
anchorage over on the shore opposite. Then I
used to go ashore to amuse myself.

One day a sou'-wester sent me ashore at Nerochóri.
Where this place is you will find out when you go
to visit Chloronísi.

As I debarked upon the jetty, thought I to myself, suppose I go and light a taper at St Nicholas'
church (St Nicholas was the patron saint of the
village, as he is of all sailors and fisher folk). Climbing the ascent, what should I see but a funeral !
They were bringing the body out of a cottage on the
outskirts of the place, and on their way to church.
A bad omen this, thought I. But God be praised, it
was an old woman they were burying. The poor
old husband followed behind, half-supported by the

people, since he could not walk by himself. Among
the mourners were some other old women, and of
men two or three. I joined myself to the company.

We entered the church. "A pretty entertain-
ment this," thought I. "Ashore for fun, and you
find a funeral! and to-night, when you want to
sleep, you'll see the whole thing before your eyes!"

St Nicholas' is the only church in the village.
It is little and low, dim and dark; the building
must be at least a hundred years old. Inside
are no pillars, and no dome above; but it is
covered with a flat roof like the houses. The
windows are small, and the floor nothing but beaten
earth. The lattice that parts off the women's
place from the men, was very thick and black with
age; and so were the stalls. A rood-screen of
walnut wood, beautifully carved, reached nearly to
the roof. Upon this you could see the church
treasure, of which the sacred picture of St Nicholas
had a larger share than our Lady. His sconce was
a huge mass of solid silver; his crowns and other
ornaments were innumerable; there were numbers
of little golden ships and anchors of gold. All but
the face of the picture was hidden under silver and
gold.

As I cast a few glances around me, they laid the
dead in the midst. For one moment the chanting

of psalms was hushed, and nothing could be heard
but the faint sputter of lamps and tapers. A chill
seemed to pass through us. When the priest began
to read his part of the service, I made an attempt
to see the old husband. A strange old man he
looked; he was trembling from head to foot, and
they had to hold him up, as though he had but
just arisen from some grievous sickness. He was
yellow, and tall for all his stoop, with bushy brows
that fell over his eyes, lips all a-tremble, hair and
moustache snow-white—a fine old man, but what a
wreck !

Half an hour later we passed out into the graveyard which lay beside the church; yet a few minutes,
and the first clods fell into the grave. Here the
old man could bear up no longer. He rolled over
upon the grass, groaned something, and never
another word said he. They sprinkled water
upon him, and raised his head, but all in vain.
Then they bore him into the priest's cell where he
half opened his eyes, cast one look at the icon of
St Nicholas, and stiffened. The old man was dead.

I left the place, and having nothing better to
do, bent my steps towards the landing-place.
Before I had got there everybody in the place had
heard the news, how Gaffer Marínos Kontáras was
dead for sorrow that he had lost his beloved Lemóne.

Taking a stool, I sat down by the sea-side; and as I sat inhaling the smoke of my narghileh, who should come up and bid me good-day, but Kapetan Thanásis. I knew the man well enough, as he often came over to our parts with fish for sale. I ordered a glass of mastick for him, and he took to it kindly, and made himself at home. One glass was nothing for him, I knew, and ordered another. Then the drams already drunk began to gossip, that other drams might follow.

He was never at a loss for something to say, was Thanasis. This time the subject was not far to seek, in the shape of Gaffer Marinos, the sea-gull of Moschonnísi, and once the terror of Anatolia. "Let's begin at the beginning," said the skipper to me, and off he goes.

"I was a bit of a lad,—cabin-boy aboard the vessel commanded by Skipper Manólis (God rest his soul), when one day up came the lugger of Marinos Kontaras. They were hunting him, God knows where, and he burrowed in here for hiding. He did not know what they wanted him for, and did not care; if it was not for murder, it was for robbery. He came with five or six cuttle-fish lying at the bottom of his boat, and a few oysters and sea-urchins, and pretended to have business on hand. A most unmanageable fellow he was; his knife was always

smeared with blood, very often with his own, for
when he got drunk he used to stick it in the
muscles to show his pluck. Plucky the devil
certainly was, and handsome too.

"No sooner had his boat come to anchor down
yonder, than out he jumped, and made straight for
the vineyard of Gligóris Physékis; ran along the
wall, picked his skirt full of grapes, and back again
as innocent as a lamb. But on the way Gligoris
met him; this man was at the time the village
champion, a terrible brawler. Well, he shouted
loud enough when he saw the thief. Kontaras
laughed, and made for his boat; Gligoris was after
him; the neighbours heard the uproar, and one by
one a crowd gathered. Marinos was by this time
sitting unconcerned in his boat, and sharing the
grapes with his mates. Our people fired up, leapt
aboard, and made as though they would lay hands
on the man. But in an instant he was up, and out
on the sand, and out flashed his knife, and says he,
'Aha, you devils! Did you never hear of Marinos
Kontaras?'

"This was a thunderclap. But Gligoris, however,
did not mean to be thwarted so easily, and then
have all the village twitting him by-and-bye, so
says he:

"'Well, if you're Marinos Kontaras, I am Gligoris

Physekis ; and if you like to measure yourself against me down with your dirk, and let's wrestle a fall here upon the sand ! '

" Marinos looked the other full in the eyes, and smiled. He doffed his vest and threw it down upon the sand, laid the dirk beside it, and began to strut about, swaying his hands as if he were going to dance. Gligoris did the same.

"'And whoever is thrown stands treat this evening all round ? '

" ' To-morrow, too ! ' says Marinos.

" ' And pays for music ? '

" ' Yes, and pays for the music ! '

" With fierce looks, they leapt upon each other. The whole thing took no longer than you might say, Amen : Kontaras got Gligoris by the waist, and laid him flat.

" ' That's enough, Gligoris ! ' cried the bystanders, ' your back has bit the dust ! '

" Gligoris got up, shook himself, put on his waistcoat, and began to think it would have been better to put up with the loss of the grapes.

" That evening, the tavern of mine host Theocháres was full of merriment. All the village was assembled outside to see the notorious Kontaras. When it was a case of ' business,' he used to be like a wild beast ; now he seemed like an angel.

Only the neighbourhood of Moschonnisi produces heroes like that! Tall as a cypress, and his waist, you might have got it through a ring; eyes big and beautiful like a girl's, and a black moustache, curled up at the ends. Everyone admired him as he sat upon his stool, and drank to the health of Gligoris. He called him comrade now, and praised the sweetness of his grapes. Gligoris on his part was proud of such a friend, the fall notwith-standing.

"—My throat feels a bit dry, sir," went on Skipper Thanasis; "I have more to tell, and I see you want to hear it."

A third glass was brought; he tossed it off at a gulp, and began again.

"They sent to Megalochori for fiddlers; and when they came, the fun grew fast and furious. Games began, songs struck up, the dancers tripped it merrily. Marinos made them get up one after another. When midnight had passed, nothing would do but they must go and serenade some-body. Straight to the house of Gligoris they went; Gligoris at that time lived with his step-mother, and his sister Lemone with him. Nothing would do for Gligoris but she must get up and mix the wine for them. The girl was awaked from her first sleep, and put on her things; for her

brother's word was law to her. There was some
one else in the crowd besides, one whom Gligoris
had in his eye as a husband for her. At last
Lemone was ready, and came out with the tray.
She was a girl of eighteen, black-eyed and golden-
haired. When they saw her, they all forgot their
fun; but the man who was most taken aback was
Marinos Kontaras. He twirled and twirled at his
moustache, pretended not to see her, but do what
he would, his eyes remained fixed upon the girl.
Gligoris, good simple fellow, noticed nothing amiss,
and besides, he did not fear the devil himself for
her. And it may be he was proud of their looking
at her so. Away went the girl, back she came again,
and once more off; till morning they kept her on
the move,—coming, going, serving.

"Songs and dances began anew, but no more
taste for follies had Marinos. He made as though
he had drunk too much and sat in a corner, where
he did nothing but twirl his moustache. You
might have thought that Satan had come up
from hell and whispered to him, so restless did
he appear.

"About dawn of day, Gligoris caught him by
the hand and whirled him into the dance again.

"'How soon the wine makes you nod, you
sailors!' said he.

"Marinos did not object; he wanted a vent for his feelings. He pulled off his scarf, and began dancing like one demented. By-and-bye he broke out into song; throwing a dollar to the fiddler, he told him what tune he wanted, and then were heard for the first time those verses which we still sing at a wedding:

> "'Black are thine eyes, and golden is thy hair;
> And for thy cheek—a golden spot is there!'

You know the air; only think of it, and off you go.—When the song ended, he fell a-thinking once more, and as he sat like this, he turned suddenly to Gligoris, and said:

"'Ah, my dear Gligoris, I can't stand it; one more glass and I'm off.'

"Gligoris, by this time as drunk as he could be, called to Lemone, and she came. That's where the mischief happened. Up got Marinos, took the glass, and looking straight at the girl, said to her, just as if they two were there alone:

> "'1 entered where the vine grows fair, to find sweet grapes
> for eating;
> Yet did not meet a thing so sweet as are thy kisses,
> sweeting!'

and as he said the words, he actually stooped down and kissed her on the lips!

"Such an insult was a thing unheard of in our honourable village. The girl blushed red, and disappeared from amongst us; she went out and sobbed like a little child. Then the mother came in for the first time, and spoke her mind to Gligoris. All the company fell silent; the musicians departed, the rest followed one by one. Gligoris was as though just awakened from a dream; one moment he looked about him, the next, he threw himself upon Marinos. Now the angel became a wild beast again. Out flashed his knife; he glared at Gligoris with the look of a devil. Two or three rushed upon him, wrenched the dagger from his hand, and dragged him outside the house; then hustling him along, they made their way towards his boat. On the way, each as he passed his home dropt in, and got pistol, or knife, or hatchet; then, arrived at the landing-stairs, they formed in line, like soldiers on parade, and shouted to him to be off with his crew, or they would send them all to the bottom. There were only a few men with Marinos, and those mostly drunk; so as needs must, he seized the pole, and in pushing off, said with a grim smile, 'To our next meeting!' The boat moved slowly over the water.

"After a little while, Gligoris made his appearance, gun in hand. Finding that the boat was away, he fell in a passion, and leapt into the water to follow her. It was but a drunkard's folly; the people fished him out, and got him home again."

At this point, old Thanasis gave me another hint. When he had wet his whistle, he began once more.

"So far, master, it's all fun; now the romance begins. What follows I didn't see with my own eyes, but I have heard it often from the man himself, who now lies dead up yonder. Marinos, as they voyaged onwards, was like a mad lion. An hour he remained silent; then he called to his men, and said to them :

"'My lads, I have saved you from many a tight place before now; to-day it's your turn to do the same by me. That girl I mean to carry off, and I mean to marry her. I have travelled, look you, through all Anatolia and the islands, looking for a woman who could kindle my heart, and never a one I found. Now I have found her at last, do you suppose I shall let her slip? Either I'll have her, or by St Nicholas, we'll perish together!'

"The lads knew that their skipper was in earnest.

"'But what if the girl won't have you?' put in one of them.

"'Won't have me, quotha! Stupid dumpling, didn't you see how she blushed when I gave her a look? Aï, you pumpkin! you talk as if you had never seen a woman. — Now we'll make for the headland yonder; by evening we are at Therma, and there we anchor. I will go ashore by myself, drest like a beggar; you wait for me by the shore.'

"And so it happened. Late in the evening, as it began to grow dark, a beggar came knocking at the door of Gligoris' house. Gligoris was making merry at the tavern; the musicians had not gone away yet. The old dame was gossiping all round the place, and the girl sat in the house alone, and cooked the supper. All that day Lemone had been overwhelmed with shame; her eyes were red with weeping. The girls of the neighbourhood were very loving, bless their kind hearts, and came one by one and vowed that never by word or song would they throw this in her teeth: it was none of her fault. The girl took their comfort, and by evening she was herself again. And she began to think how much better it would have been to declare his love like a man, poor fellow. A word or two would have persuaded Gligoris. But now there was an end of it all. She would never see him again, never hear his voice. Just at that moment came the knock.

"'Who's there?' cried the girl, within.

"'May the blessed God forgive thy dead, my daughter; the world I hear, but the world I cannot see; have pity, and give me an alms of thy charity!'

" The door opened ; the girl's hand held out a piece of bread.

" ' God forgive thy dead !' murmured Marinos once more, and in he stept. Lemone knew him instantly, and fell in a faint. There was no time to lose. One glance Marinos threw around, then whipt off his scarf, and bound it over her mouth ; he lifted her on his shoulders, got across the yard and over the back wall, landing in some rubbish-heaps ; thence he made his way across one field, across a second field, and pausing at length, sat down under a tree. Now he sprinkled her face with some orange-flower water which he had with him. She half opened her eyes, and Marinos saw there was no danger. He next fastened the bandage over her mouth again, and then straight away for the boat.

" The lads were all ready, resting on their oars, and in half an hour they had got as far as Kalo-chori. As they went, the girl came to ; but God knows how she felt. Marinos treated her as a mother would treat her first - born child. He spoke to her, made her promises, fondled her, with never a hard word said, and never a hard thing done. By degrees the girl began to breathe easier ; it was as if her heart told her a thing that calmed her mind. Suddenly it all came

E

over her at once : her home, her brother, her native
village, her shame. Ah ! the shameful ditty they
would make about her. Again she fainted ; another
dose of orange-water, and the same pitiful scene
was repeated. When she was more herself, Marinos
(who knew what was troubling her) began to plead
once more, and in sweet words told her that he
would not lay a finger upon her until they should
be wed ; nor should they be wed until she said yes,
and his lads for witness. They had arrived at
Kalochori, and still Lemone never opened her lips.
Marinos now reminded her that there was no time
for thinking ; here they were. At this the girl
burst into lamentations. However, as the men held
fast by the boat-hook while they got out on the beach
down behind the harbour, she called out, and said :

" ' If you will take an oath before the Virgin
and St Nicholas, and before the priest, that your
life, now and for ever, shall be gentle and sweet as
the words you have said to me ; that you will renounce the sea and renounce the knife ; and that
you will return to our village with the priest, to
bear witness that he received me with my honour
unstained ; and if you will live with me always,
my answer is—Yes.'

" Marinos wanted nothing else ; he was ready to
swear anything if he might win her love.

" So they left the boat, and passing through the dark streets, arrived before the Church. They found the priest's cell, and called up the curate to explain what they required. At first the curate refused to be mixed up in the matter, but when he saw that there were knives ready to enforce the request, how could he help it ? So he got out his stole, and made them one. Before the blessing, the oath was twice taken : once upon the Gospel, and once before St Nicholas, whom Marinos feared a great deal more than he feared the Gospel.

" ' Now,' says Marinos, ' back we go, priest and all.' And one hour before dawn the vessel came to anchor in our harbour. The sailors were well armed, in case of mischief, if our people got wind of them. First went the priest alone, and he went to the house of Gligoris. Oh, the trouble there had been in the place ! All through the night they had been afoot ; all night long there had been search-parties with lanterns looking for the runaway ; and they were just arranging to send men round to all the villages for them to seek for the lost Lemone.

" But the priest made it all straight with them. When he got inside, he went straight to the girl's brother, who was at that time sitting with his cheeks in his two hands, and his elbows on his knees, staring before him fiercely, like a madman ; and to him said the priest :

" ' My son, the blessing of God be with thee ; fear nothing. Thy sister is at this hour chaste and pure as the day when she was born. He who carried her off is a changed man. See, here is his oath. If thou canst not read, I will read it to thee :

" ' I swear by the Gospel and by St Nicholas (great is his grace), that from the hour when I take Lemone, daughter of Mastro-Vasili, of Nero-chori, to be my wife, until the day of my death, I will renounce the sea, I will not touch a knife, I will live with her in Nerochori, I will never say her a bitter word, but I will live and die by her side in peace and love.'

' MARINOS KONTARAS.'

Gligoris foamed with rage when he heard this. Then the burly priest, who had seen the world in his day, bade all the others go out and leave them together. A whole hour they remained alone. Gligoris cried aloud, and beat his breast, and the priest gently rebuked him. At last when the dawn came, we who were outside heard the noise grow less, then the sound of voices in talk together ; and finally, as the sun caught the headland over yonder across the bay, out came the priest, Gligoris, and all

the family, and with some of the neighbours and
the musicians in front, marched down to the sea-
shore to escort the bride home.

"When the fiddlers appeared, followed by this
wedding procession, Marinos and his men began to
weep like little children for very joy, Lemone could
hold up no longer, and fainted away; this time it
was Gligoris sprinkled the orange-water to revive
her, and led her ashore.

"The whole village was crowding on the beach
by this time, and we all struck up the *Bride's Song*.
Never shall I forget that march from the sea-shore
up to the village. First of all we went to St
Nicholas' Church, and there Marinos made a vow
to sell his boat, and offer with the money a silver
sconce, the same you must have seen up in the
church to-day.

"The service over, they returned home; the
women gathered together and dressed the bride,
and then came the wedding feast. A topsy-turvy
wedding it was, to be sure—crowning first and feast
after! Half the night the revelry lasted. I was
there at the dance myself, a beardless boy, my first
wedding dance, so I remember it all the better.
But how shall I ever get to the end of my story,
sir?"

I begged old Thanasis to tell me no more to-day,

as it was getting late, and I must be off. I ordered him another dram, and bade good-night.

"But you haven't heard all yet, sir! You haven't heard what became of the wild beast when he was turned into an angel! What bliss he had with his Lemone, and the vineyard Gligoris gave them! How for years he would not even fish, until the priest of Kalochori, who had married them, came saying that he had seen St Nicholas in a dream, angry because Marinos did no more fishing! And after that he began to take out his drag-net now and again to catch fish for his beloved wife.

"In a word, master, fifty years they lived thus, loving and beloved, and so they have died this day. One sorrow they had, and one only; and that was that they had no children. But every other joy that life can give was theirs. 'Twas the will of God that his soul should be saved by a girl—a woman! And yet they do say that women cause our damnation! But you see, sir, there are women and women. Just look now at that old beldame of mine, and say whether I'm right to spend my evenings at the tavern?"

"Well, good evening, skipper. I must go light a taper and be off, or I shall catch it, too, from my wife, if I'm very late."

And so I got up and left him.

Once more I entered the church. There was an hour or so left ere sunset. In the burial ground all was still. The door was shut, and neither priest nor grave-digger was to be seen. I went in, and walked to the grave of Lemone. There were two graves now, side by side, and upon them lay the pick and shovel, forming a rude cross. Over the graves I bent my head, and prayed to God to fill the world with such couples as these, who begin their life with a loving kiss, and go down into the grave hand in hand.

ZANOS CHARISIS

ZÁNOS CHARÍSIS was a lively boy; very lively. Komnenós Verníkis was his inseparable friend, from the time when they used to twist up wisps of hay, and smoke them on the sly down the garden. Zanos was a restless boy; a "prankish lad," as they say in the island where he lived, about any boy who afterwards makes a figure in the world.

People noticed these pranks of Zanos, and they were the talk of the place. But that fine widow lady, his mother, who, ever since she had lost her mate after one year of bliss, lavished all her love on this yellow-haired lump of a lad, could see below the surface. She saw that her Zanos had his father's head, all his tastes, his quickness, and his fire. She saw that one day he too would love; and that love, if it were unhappy, would break his heart, or else, if it were wise and not unrequited, would spring within it like a fountain of living water.

Another thing that helped Charisena to understand her boy was his affection for Komnenos. Komnenos was rather bigger than he, a little

heavy, but wide-awake for all that. He was a
deep stream, this doctor's son, and eminently
practical. He weighed well all that he said or did.
When Zanos proposed some piece of madness or
practical joke, Komnenos would carefully deliberate
the matter, and then pronounce sentence. These
two were the torment and terror of the whole
neighbourhood. Once old Aunt Ralou found some
of the strings of the warp cut in a piece of work she
was doing. Cries and imprecations burst from her
lips, and there was a regular row. But she did not
need to wonder who did it. Off she ran post-
haste to Charisena's yard, and called her with uplifted hands: not a sound, no one answered. By-
and-bye in came Zanos, as innocent as you please,
bearing a basket of fruit, as if it was likely he
would come back from the garden at that time of
day. A question, and the whole thing came out at
once. The youngster could not lie, and was not
afraid to tell the truth. What could Aunt Ralou
do but catch him and give him a kiss?

.   .   .   .   .

Playtime ended and school began. Our two
friends went to school together. Komnenos began
to work hard at once; slow but sure, he learnt
everything. The other, rogue that he was, took
all his pranks to school with him. The master

could not help loving a lad so sweet-tempered, and
had not the heart to punish him. And then the
boy did no harm; only, keep quiet he could not.
His mind swung to and fro like his feet as he sat
upon the form. He never knew any lesson
thoroughly, and all he learnt was by fits and starts
and on the move.

Yet great and marvellous are the miracles
worked by school. After a few years, the lad was
promoted to the higher classes, with much pride
and complacency; always in company with Komnenos. But what a difference there was now!
One got on at a run, the other at a slow walk.
Zanos now and then stopt still by the way and
waited for his friend, and so the two schoolboy
chums were not separated.

.   .   .   .   .

Zanos must have grown by this time to the age
of fifteen or so; an awkward age, when a boy
becomes a nuisance, neither fish nor flesh, and his
voice as much as the rest of him. Someone has
said that at this age boys ought to be hidden under
a barrel, so that nobody need see them; but Dame
Charisena was not of this opinion. She longed for
the day when her boy would be a man. What
other hope in the world had she? And as she saw
him develop by slow degrees, joy and hope over-

flowed her heart. She had her own little fortune,
more than enough for their needs. All her ambi-
tion was for his advancement, that he should come
to the front and be a famous man. She wished to
hear once more the sweet name of Charísis ringing
round her, and to see her lost husband live again in
her son.

Two or three years more, and half her wish was
fulfilled; now she must work for the other half.
A budding moustache was not enough; he must
become a personage. For this end she had been
striving until now with her love and her sweet
words. But she could not carry it through herself; Zanos had to go abroad, to travel and see the
world, and to enter some profession. The only pro-
fessions that families of any importance would look
at then were medicine and the law. To be a
barrister was no wish of his, neither would his
mother have allowed it, for she would have lost
him then from her village home. So there was
nothing for it but to become a doctor. Old Vernikis, the father of Komnenos, now cared more for
his crops than his patients, and so disgusted was
he at being for ever at beck and call, day or night,
that he would not hear of the profession of medicine for his son. Go to Athens—yes, he might go
to Athens, if he liked; and be what he would, but

not a doctor. Komnenos might become a lawyer, a bishop, a schoolmaster; but no—he wanted none of them. What he liked was to be out of doors; his father's son all over. So he decided to give himself to farming.

   .   .   .   .   .

It was the end of August. The two families were supping together on the eve of the departure. The boxes were already packed, with lavender and acacia seeds folded away among the clothes to scent them; a few kerchiefs and little bags full of souvenirs were all made up. The young folks seemed glad; the mothers thoughtful. They were on the brink of tears, but weeping was left for the morrow.

Old Vernikis that night was full of instructions for their benefit. There was no piece of information he forgot to give, no old friend he did not call to mind, no introduction he failed to offer.

Supper done, Vernikis' wife had still something to finish, which she was weaving for her Komnenos. And that little birdie of hers, Chrysoula, flitted about, coming and going, each time with some new trifle, this or that, which must go in Komnenos' box.

Charisena had nothing left to do. All Zanos' things had been ready for days and days past. What else had she had to think about all these

years? So she lent a hand to the other, and gave
her opinion on the ten thousand things the wee
lassie had to offer.

And so the evening passed. Very early in the
morning, Charisena strolled round the garden with
Komnenos, while Zanos saw after the horses. They
talked together, these two, very seriously. Komnenos
carried his head like a full-grown man, and Zanos'
mother talked and talked, now bright and laughing,
and again in a quiet and confidential fashion: they
seemed to be hatching some plan between them.
Her expression was unusually knowing, as who
should say: "We have business on hand." In
a little while came Mistress Vernikena,[1] with her
husband, and joined in. So it was no new thing,
this little plan of theirs.

Suddenly the horses were heard in the courtyard.
They must start at once if they would catch the
steamer; there was no time to lose. Zanos, too,
was a sensitive lad; and though his heart grieved
at leaving his dear mother for the first time, he
longed to be gone, and the pain of parting over.
At last all was ready. They embraced, and for one
moment the mothers were locked in their sons'
arms, without a word of complaint, only cries and
sobs. Even the doctor broke down, and two big

---

[1] *I.e.*, Vernikis' wife, as Charisis' wife is Charisena.

drops rolled over his cheeks as he kissed the young
fellows. Suddenly they remembered that Chrysoula
was not there. Her father called her; Komnenos
called her. At last there she came, running out of
the garden, with two bunches of flowers in her hand:
one for her brother, one for Zanos. Then followed
more tears, more kisses. At length the gates
opened, and the horses passed out; the men pulled
them forward, followed by the two travellers, the
mothers next, and finally, a procession of friends
and neighbours. " Farewell, farewell!" cried they
all; only the mothers found no voice. However,
Charisena managed to control herself so far as to
say two words apart to her son. " No fear, no fear!"
he answered, smiling; then the beasts and travellers
turned the corner, and proceeded on their way.

A few moments more, and nothing was to be
seen in the distance but handkerchiefs fluttering in
the air.

．　　　．　　　．　　　．　　　．

A week or so later, Zanos' mother received the
following letter :—

" MY DEAR MOTHER,—

" If we go on as we have begun, we shall do
well. Our journey was quiet and sweet as a dream.
Only, whenever I thought of you, and——but

didn't I say all would end well? Then where's the use of sitting down to lament now? Courage, and the years will fly.

" What a fine town Athens is! I only wish you were here to see it. Perhaps even that may come to pass! Well, never mind that just now. Komnenos is always dinning into my ears that 'we have not come here to make our bed,' and 'there's nothing like a home-made boot, even if it is patched.' You know his proverbs. What amuses me is, that you sent me here to work hard, and then it suddenly comes into your head to talk of wives and weddings! But there—you mothers will never learn sense. I'll tell you what I mean to do. I'll make up your advice into a neat parcel, and put it carefully away until I am a doctor, and then we'll talk of it again. Is that a bargain?

" To-morrow we begin our studies. We have settled down very comfortably in two rooms, Komnenos and I. Give my love to all.—Your

" ZANOS."

Not twenty-four hours elapsed before Zanos himself was reading a letter, which ran thus—

" MY DARLING ZANOS,—

" I can't tell you how dreary the house has been ever since you went away. You will begin to

scold me, I know. . . . You promised me that
you would remain faithful to your word. In God's
name, my son, do not break that vow! My dream
is that you will come back one day, and take your
father's place. I found a wife for you before you
left us; you know who. Don't tell me again that
it is too soon yet. There is plenty of time, my
boy, for you to work and to love Chrysoula; and
when you have her to love, you will learn all the
quicker. The poor little thing seems to have
suspected something from our mysterious whispers,
and every little while she keeps asking when your
letters will come. Perhaps we shall have them to-
morrow morning. I am going to bed, after a
fervent prayer for my dear son.

"YOUR MOTHER."

"P.S.—It was lucky that I did not send my
letter yesterday. To-day yours has come. Imagine
our delight! Just look at my letter, and be duly
astonished that I wrote as though I knew what
you were writing to me! We have made our
bargain, then; God be praised for it. If I lose
not thee, my son, the world may come to an end
for all I care."

Six months went by; twelve months. Zanos by
this time was rising twenty, Komnenos was twenty-

one. Komnenos, though, was still as cool as ever ;
you must push him if you would move him.
Zanos was exactly the opposite. He took fire like
powder whenever a petticoat trailed across his path.
It was vacation time now, and the two used to go
out together for a good walk every evening, when
work was done. Their plan was to work right
through the vacation, that so they might shorten
their exile. So they set their teeth, and stayed
away from home those two or three months, cost
what it might to poor Charisena.

To be young and handsome, to be Zanos, and to
see, look you, every evening a witch with hazel
eyes who passes you with a smile—this methinks
were temptation enough to move even St Anthony.
This was what happened to Zanos. At first he
took the whole thing as a bit of fun, and joked
over it with Komnenos. And perhaps it would
have stopped there, but that for a few days
Komnenos was ill. Then Zanos had to take his
walk by himself. That was too much for his
blood. At first he was devoured by curiosity.
Who could she be? How well she dressed, and
sometimes she was on horseback, too! "Ah, take
care, beware, Zanos!" he said once to himself,
"she's fooling thee! What pluck, though, to turn
the horse right round and make eyes at me! She

must be a boy, not a girl. Who *can* she be, though?"

By hook or by crook, he discovered that she was the only daughter of Siour[1] Pezoúlis, who had come last year from Europe to settle in Athens. Then he held up his head with a knowing air, as who should say, let this foreign girl try her game somewhere else. But in his heart of hearts he flattered his hopes, and was proud of the experience. When he got home, he asked Komnenos how he was getting on, and advised him like a good doctor to take care of himself, and not to go out just yet; then hastened to his room. But now his head began to turn, and he could get no rest.

"Hang it all!" he said suddenly, half-aloud, "I'm young, and I must amuse myself. It's not a question of marrying, anyhow, or of being false to mother. Poor mother!"

Opening his drawer he drew out one by one all his little treasures; crosses, dried flowers, handkerchiefs, all came out. He looked at them each one, folded them up again carefully and mechanically, as if in a dream, and went to bed. As he lay in his bed, his heart was groaning, while fancy played her own tune upon it; yet his mind was awake, exultant. He began to toss from side to side,

---

[1] A corruption of *Signor*.

trying to devise some excuse for calling upon Siour
Pezoulis. Was he to deny himself all the pleasures
of life ? What sort of man was he then ? And what
virtue could there be, if there were no temptations
to overcome ? Besides, the world was not learnt
from books, and a good doctor must know the world.

Soothed with sophistries like these, he fell asleep.
In the morning he paid his friend another visit.
Komnenos regarded him cool as ever, and showed
not the slightest curiosity ; but he guessed there
was something afoot. And when Zanos again insisted that he must not think of going out that
day, he was sure of it.

Late that evening Zanos returned, in hot haste,
like a hare before the hunters. That is what high-
strung temperaments are like when they catch fire.
And why not ? He had been received at Pezoulis'
house like one of the family. A fine old fellow he
was, to be sure : but his daughter———! How in-
telligent she was, how delicately she spoke ! And
to think that we boast of our island girls, and say
we know something of the world ! What fine
manners she had, what wit and grace ! She tells
you a mere nothing, and honey trickles from her
lips. And she too was an island girl, she said ;
from Chios. Now tell me, mother mine ; " what
hae ye to say for yoursel' ? "

So he made a joke of it in his thoughts; perhaps he really did think it a joke still. His laugh, however, as he entered Komnenos' chamber was rather forced; and when his friend asked him had he seen Hazel-eyes that evening, the laugh grew rigid, lifeless, mere mummery.

Komnenos had no difficulty in dragging the snake from its hole. Two or three questions, and Zanos made a clean breast of it, so that the other saw his heart to the bottom. He perceived that it was grim earnest now. There was no longer time to pretend to feel worse, and say he must go home for a few weeks; work would soon begin again. Now, he considered, some other antidote must be found, and it was time to put a certain little plot into execution. He passed the matter off as a fine joke, and the evening went by.

.   .   .   .   .

Of course the letters came and went all this time. Zanos wrote every Sunday; and his mother wrote something every day, sending off the budget as soon as it was full. Like fresh flowers were his mother's letters to Zanos; like healing balm were his to her: those, sunbeams warming an exiled heart; these, a mirror that reflected that heart with all its beauties and all its faults. Then how could Zanos help telling his mother his adventure with the brown-eyed

lass? Tell it he did, as something quite delightful.
What else could it be but delightful? However,
Charisena understood it rather better than Komnenos. "Time for the 'ruse,'" his letter said, just
at the end.

Five or six days had gone by without Zanos
meeting his Dulcinea at Patissia; and yet he always went at the same hour. Zanos began to feel
uneasy. Perhaps she preferred meeting him alone.
But how was he to get rid of Komnenos? It was
impossible to look wise, and tell him to stay indoors. He had not even a cold now.

One evening, seeing his friend very restless,
Komnenos said:

"Suppose we go to the theatre?"

"So we will!" cried Zanos, at once. He was
charmed with the idea. What a fool he had been
not to think of that! His lady-love was sure to be
there; an opera was running such as could not be
seen every day.

In half an hour they were sitting in the theatre
side by side. Zanos could not keep his eyes still.
One comprehensive glance took in the whole audi-
ence; curse it, there was no sign of Signor Pezoulis.
Did but a door open, did anyone come in, Zanos
was all eyes: but nothing came of it. "We shan't
see her to-night!" he murmured to himself.

The performance ended, and they made their way home. They talked of the music, of this, that, and the other; Komnenos was more lively than usual, and even struck up a song, while Zanos sat still and listened.

"Let us have that again," said he; it was the air sung by the tenor, which Zanos liked very much.

All of a sudden, Komnenos went off into one of their island songs.

"Ugh, you wretch, you haven't a particle of taste," said Zanos. "Your heart is wood, nothing but wood!" and he got up and stalked off to his room.

Next day all went on as usual; work, dinner, a short nap, and then their walk. As they walked, suddenly Komnenos called out—

"There she is!"

"Where?" cried Zanos. But this "where?" sharp as a pistol-shot, was heard by other ears as well; she of the hazel eyes heard it; she turned, and gave him a sweet look. Zanos turned from pale to red, and greeting her with some awkwardness, began to walk like one possessed. So much had this little incident confused him that he went straight ahead, not looking to the right hand nor to the left. Komnenos had a great mind to tease him, only he knew that it is ill jesting with men in love; so he let the cloud pass by.

Slowly, by degrees, Zanos recovered, and became quieter and more reasonable. " I'm very glad she heard me," he was thinking. " She must have seen my heart in that word. My heart!" he went on ; " it's not a question of heart ; of course I must have perceived her beauty ; how could I help it ? " And thus he laid unction to his conscience, that he might have uo need to hide anything from his mother.

On the way home, Komnenos stayed behind to buy something, and so Zanos went on by himself. He threw down his hat upon the table ; and just as he did so, a large square envelope caught his eye ; the postman had just brought it in, said the landlady. It was directed in a thin, clear hand. He stood looking at it as he drew off his gloves, and tried to guess who had sent it. Suddenly he heard Komnenos coming ; catching up the letter, he hastened to his own room, and locked the door. Then he opened it and began to read.

" I have often thought of writing to you. Yesterday was not the first time I have seen you. And now I am going to forget that I am a girl, a mere school-girl indeed, and that I run a thousand risks in taking this step. Risks ? what do I care for risks ? what do I care for my life ? Mine it is no longer, and alas ! I cannot call it yours. I dare

not even say who I am. Why should I write a
name which I want no longer? And how can I
tell that you will not think me crazy? Who ever
heard of such a thing—that a girl should write to
a young man and a stranger, to say, and to be the
first to say it, 'I love you'! Sweet, sweet word,
which I now write for the first time, with such
passion; I feel it in my heart, I know what it
means, and I will write it. I shall perish if I write
it not. You know not who I am, perhaps never
will,—never! But you shall know that there is a
girl who loves you so deeply that she has lost her
reason for your sake.

" Now I have told you : but where is the use ?
What man will ever listen to a girl whom he cannot
see and does not know? And who would believe
her if she said—no, I will never write it. I have
shown you my heart, it is enough. If my heart's
cries find an echo in yours—but impossible ! All
you need know is that you are loved as never man
was loved yet, and that there lives a girl who one
day will die for love of you.

" P.S.—*If* you care to answer me, it is enough to
wear a white flower in your coat."

Very slowly he folded the letter, and sat down to
think. He did not know what to make of it. For a

moment the thought crossed his mind that this was some practical joke. He looked at the letter again ; no, that would not do : the words were a woman's, it was a woman's handwriting ; the very perfume of the paper showed that some woman had sent it.

"I say, how much longer am I to wait for you?" called the voice of Komnenos, outside.

"Don't wait; I have a headache this evening, and I am not coming. I think I shall go to bed." And to bed he went, cudgelling his brains to think who the girl could be. Hazel-eyes it certainly was not; besides, he had seen her writing in a book, and it was quite different.

"What a fool I am!" he cried, suddenly. "It's just what the letter says, some girl who has taken a fancy to me. But I'm not to write to her! a white flower is enough! And what would she understand by that? Perhaps she would write again. What if it's a trap, though, and they will look out for the white flower and laugh at me! No, I'll do nothing at all till she writes again. I will wait. But I might tell Komnenos. Happy thought; he will know if it's a joke. Ah, there's mother; what would she say about it? Well, she shall be told too. I can't help it if the girls write me letters. I never saw this poor little girl, and don't know who she is. Certainly I will write and tell mother. At least it will give her a laugh ; at most she will give me a warning."

Accordingly, next morning, as Zanos was drinking his coffee, he handed the letter to Komnenos, with the words, " Read this, and give me your opinion."

Komnenos read it through. When he had finished, he knit his brows and thought a moment. Then he said :

" Why, what am I to say ? It's some girl who is in love with you. Is that what made you unwell yesterday ? You are not to blame."

" What would you do if you were in my place ? " asked Zanos.

" Why, what *can* you do ? unless you want to humour the girl, and put a white flower in your button-hole. That means you say yes ; and then, get out of it if you can ! That would make matters serious ; look before you leap."

" You're quite right ; I will do nothing. Still, I'll send the letter to mother, that she may enjoy the joke ; what do you think ? "

" No harm in that ;—yes, you had best send it, and show her that you are just the same as ever."

.   .   .   .   .   .

As the days passed, Zanos became shy. He fed his mind on study, and his heart on love ; and now that Komnenos knew the secret, his love had to be

kept to himself. So he used to retire very early
to his room, to think of his "little girl" (as he
called her). As for Hazel-eyes, he never gave her
a look now.

A week or so later, a letter came from his mother.
"We had a good laugh," so it began, "over the
billet doux of your unknown fair one. If I did not
know your heart, I should feel anxious. May all
your temptations be no worse than this, my boy,
and then I have no fear of losing you."

"You see she takes it as a trifle," said he, on
showing this to his friend.

"Well, how did you expect her to take it? you
told it her yourself for a bit of fun. That's what
we ought to have thought of it all along. A school-
girl babbling of love, indeed! An unfledged chick
dreaming of the sky. Don't imagine that this
madness has lasted. I assure you that you might
wear your white flower to-day, and she would never
write you a line!"

Zanos, though somewhat shaken, did not feel
quite so certain that his friend was right. It
seemed to him the best plan to wear a flower,
and see whether he would get another letter.
So half in fun he bought a white camellia, put
it in his button-hole, and went for a walk.

The evening passed without events; but Zanos

was conning the girl's letter in his mind, impatient for the morning.

Early next day, after his first lecture, he came in and saw that the letter had come. It was the same envelope and directed in the same hand. Zanos trembled. His friend was smoking, and looking out of the window. By-and-bye he turned round, and said to Zanos :

"Come, read it out; let us hear what she says."

Zanos was silent. He read the document through once, and pretended to read it again, while he thought what he should say. The girl had been dying of grief because her dear one did not wear the flower, but she was better now. Yet still no name or address ! She had thought it over, and decided not to make herself known until she was done with school, and Zanos had finished his studies. Meanwhile he should get acquainted with her by degrees from her letters. She would write once a month. One favour alone she asked him ; to send her some little keepsake that she might treasure up ; if he wished for one, he had the letters. Let him direct it to such and such a name at the post office, to be called for. He might write, if he wished, just that once, a word or two ; but this would be the first and last time she meant to go to the post, so he might spare himself the trouble of writing again. For her the flower was enough, which told her that she was beloved. She had thought long whether she should send him her picture, and had decided not to do so. He had the picture of her heart, and that must do. Never should it be said that he had chosen her for a pretty face. And so it went on.

"Here," said Zanos at last; "take it and read it."

Komnenos read the letter, and turned towards the window. Then he whistled a few notes, and ended by saying:

"I was wrong in letting you wear that flower. She took it seriously, and you can't get out of it. Your mother little thought that things would go so far."

At this, Zanos burst out into a torrent of excited words. "I'll tell you what," said he, "I have had enough of it. It's high time my mother should know that I am not tied to her apron-strings any longer. I am a man now, and I mean to go my own way. I dare say I am blind, but I won't be led about by the hand; I had rather go my own way and fall into the ditch. I'm in love with the girl, so have done. I know that I am speaking to Chrysoula's brother; but Chrysoula's brother is also my friend. I mean to find out who this is, and if

I can't find out now, I shall wait until I do. If I
like the girl as well as I like her letters, she's mine,
and there's an end of it. I will write and tell
mother the same."

.   .   .   .   .

" My boy," wrote Charisena, a fortnight later,
" I see things have taken a serious turn, and day
or night I think of nothing else. What to write
to you, I know not. If I refuse my consent, I
make you unhappy—you, for whose happiness I
have given my whole life. If I agree, I lose you.
It is a terrible choice, and may God have pity on
me. At least, listen to this one prayer from your
mother; keep your heart your own till you have
seen her ; and when you have seen her, and got to
know her, if you still care for her and she is a
respectable girl, do not let your heart yield until
she gives her word that she will come here, and be
my daughter before she becomes your wife. If not,
I will never, never consent ; and it would be
better for me a thousand times to go down alive
into the grave."

This letter nearly drove Zanos wild with delight.
He did not know what to do first—whether to
adore his mother for raising him to the seventh
heaven, when he looked for adjurations and tears ;
or to pray God that he would make all work for

the best, and persuade the girl to come to his home and be his own.

" But the keepsake ! " he said suddenly. " And in the letter I will tell her all. My first love-letter, and perhaps my last ! "

He sat down, and wrote a long, long letter. Without a picture, he said, he could see her clearly before his eyes ; such a soul needed no pictures ; he loved her for better and for worse ; that he would listen to her advice, he would rest quiet, and work, and with his beloved in his heart would await the " fulness of time." He had only one boon to pray. And then he suggested the com-pact of which his mother had written. They must build their nest in his own country, by his mother's side. If her parents would not agree she must persuade them ; and if it was impossible to win their consent, they must do without, and get away as quietly as they could.

All night long he wrote. Ever and anon he would lie down ; then rise and add something more. At last he folded the letter, and placed his keep-sake in it; a golden cross, one of his mother's treasures. To what better hands could he entrust it !

Even Komnenos at last began to take him seriously. True it is, that for a time he pretended

to be grieved at losing the hope that Zanos would
marry his sister ; but by degrees it grew clear that
he loved his friend well enough to forget that.
He went so far as to buy the flowers. " Don't
forget the flower," he used to say, " you mustn't
let the poor girl go and get ill."

Zanos could not find words to praise him ; he
was brother, friend, hero. All his little efforts to
give pleasure were pure gold to Zanos, under love's
magic.

The girl's answer came. It was a letter no
longer, but a starry heaven that unfolded and shone
before him. All his conditions were accepted. She
had told her mother all. What scenes there had
been !—all that he should hear some time. Let
him rest assured that now her mother was won ;
she saw that it was a question of life and death,
and took it on herself to make all right with the
father. What a blessing that they knew who
Zanos was ! The cross she had kissed, and hung
it about her neck. She went back to her studies
with a light heart, longing for the two or three
years to pass. She had not told him how highly
he was spoken of in society ; that she had learnt
from her mother. Everybody had some kind thing
to say of him. What would they say if they
knew that Zanos was her own, hers for ever !

And now he must not forget her first request—
diligence, industry, patience: the years would soon
go by.

It was odd that on that very day an invitation
came from Hazel-eyes; they were giving a dance.
But Zanos cared nothing for such things now; he
sat down and wrote that he was indisposed.

Quietly and happily the winter went by. Zanos
and Komnenos were in great request. "Good
stuff in the lads," people said of them, "but they
have not been much in society." You see Komnenos cared little about society; give him his roots
to grub, and he was happy enough. Zanos again,
when he received one letter from his lady-love,
began to count how many days must pass before
the next came; and each evening, when work was
done, he would open the last letter and read it
through again. Sometimes he made a copy of it
for his mother, that she too might be proud of the
treasure he had found.

Month by month Zanos saw the writer's mind
grow and improve. She changed from girl to
woman, and he was very proud of her.

"Why, look here!" said he once to Komnenos,
"just see how cleverly she writes! You must read it.
Verses now, the silly girl! and not at all bad verses
either. She says she does not like the kind of

G

poetry they learn in school; it reminds her of the
artificial flowers in her hat! Real flowers are nicer,
says she! So they are, little one; we'll pull in the
same boat there! In the last letter she wrote about
our language; she wants to see it fresh, full of the
mountain air. Do not the violets smell sweet upon
the mountains?—Yes, my darling; and so they do
in Athens, sometimes!"

Komnenos listened quietly, and laughed.

"Ah, you're a lucky dog!" said he. "But if she
turns out to be ugly—what then?"

"Ugly! an ugly woman never had a soul like
that! What she says is enough to show that she
is beautiful!"

Spring passed pleasantly enough. When summer
came, again they discussed the question should they
go home or no. Travelling was easier now. But
the decision lay with Komnenos, and he decided
not to go; three summers of work would shorten
their absence by a year.

. . . . .

The third year was passed more slowly, and with
some impatience; the fourth was worse still. Zanos
was suffering from mental fever; the days seemed
to drag till he could see his "dear little girl."
Little was hardly the word for her now, he thought.
All those years he had kept a diary for her; and in
it he told her everything.

At length the last month came. The diary was bound up, and made a beautiful volume; another volume was made of the love-letters. He passed his examination with flying colours.

"I saw you," she wrote; "I saw you come out a full-fledged doctor with your diploma. I felt as proud of you as if I were already your wife. I wonder how I kept myself from running up to kiss you! My mother gave me strength. Six months more I have to stay at school, and I have been making my trousseau! What a good wife I shall make you in your island home!

"P.S. I kept this letter a day or two, in order to tell you our final plans. We have decided that the meeting shall take place *at your home*. I wish your mother to see me first, that she may give me to her son. At first I said no, but my father and mother insisted. When I remembered that but for them I should never, never have seen you, I constrained my heart, and said, So be it. I know this will grieve you. Patience, my love, only a little while, and you will see us in your own house. We leave to-night; the other steamer sails to-morrow. Take care not to lose it. We shall soon meet. Good-bye."

.   .   .   .   .

The steamer cast anchor in the bay; and the

first to leap into the boat were our two friends. It was night; and before taking the news up to the village—an hour's walk from the harbour—the travellers knocked at Charisena's door. She opened it herself; in a moment Zanos was locked in her arms.

"How changed you are, my boy!" she said, when Zanos at length had time to look round. "Why, there's Komnenos. What are you waiting for? Run, run and go to your mother! Stay, let us all go together. The bride and her family are all up there. Everybody is charmed with them."

Zanos gave a sigh of relief. His dream was true, then! The lady-love was no toy of the fancy. No doubt they arrived in the other boat, and now they were spending the evening at the doctor's.

Their arrival was a veritable triumphal march; what rejoicings there were, and how happy the people seemed to see them! They entered the courtyard, and Vernikena was out in a moment, with her arms round her son's neck; the doctor, who was too feeble to rise, shouted his welcome from within.

"Why, where's Chrysoula?" said Zanos; his tongue refused to utter any other name, so he asked for Chrysoula. He spoke with an air of some impatience, as much as to say — "Just like a girl — they always must go and put on their finery!"

"Coming, coming!" cried old Vernikis. And suddenly on the threshold appeared Chrysoula, radiant and graceful, island beauty coupled with the refinement that comes of travel and education. But surely that could not be Chrysoula? that must be his lady-love? At the mere thought, a thrill ran through the limbs of Zanos; at the same moment his mother put her arm about the girl, saying—

"This is your love, this is the 'little one'!"

Zanos could hardly believe his ears; feeling quite dazed, he came near and kissed her. Then he looked at her face once more, holding her hand and trying to speak; slowly she pulled out a golden chain that hung round her neck, and from her bosom drew out his mother's golden cross. Zanos could doubt no longer; it was she, it was she indeed! He gazed upon her with wide eyes, trying to quench that burning thirst that had racked him four long years; and he drank in her beauty as a thirsty wayfarer drinks of the spring.

He would have spoken but could not; he trembled like an aspen leaf; they were all trembling.

"I say!" called the old man's voice, "why don't you all come in?"

Zanos awoke from his dream, and turning, saw

his mother in tears, weeping for her great joy. They entered the house; Komnenos ran up to kiss his father's hand, and then he embraced the beautiful girl.

At last Zanos understood the truth. The dear little girl of his letters was Chrysoula herself! He was speechless, his throat was parched; a cloud came over him; he was far, far away, not living upon the earth.

Charisena broke the spell. "Tell me now, my boy, for the love of God, did you imagine your darling more beautiful than she is?"

Then at last Zanos understood his mother, and knew the anxiety that had been preying upon her; it was done in a moment. No, the unknown fair one could not be fairer than the maiden who there stood smiling at him. But then those letters—who wrote them? Why, Chrysoula! She was the little one, the darling; it was her sweet soul had enchanted him all these years. "Mother," he murmured, "you are right: she is an angel! she is my love!"

"Well, my children," broke in the old man, "sit down and rest a little. See how happily all has turned out! You are the happiest couple in all the world. The property is yours; Komnenos will arrange all that. He says he will bring some more

for himself. It is good that it should be so ; may
we live to see it done. There is only one thing I
fear—that you will not be allowed to enjoy your
first happiness in peace, as all the village is ill, in
fact at death's door ; there's not a doctor in the
place, only a quack fellow. We'll have the wedding
on Sunday, eh ? what say you, Charisena ? "

All was arranged, and the wedding took place.
The library of Zanos is now adorned by three gilt-
bound volumes, two of them full of manuscript, and
the third white as their own two hearts. In this
will be one day written the history of their true
love.

FIRST LOVE

I MUST have been about twelve years old, and she was about eleven. I did not meet her at church, nor on St John's Eve, when the girls look for omens, nor at the spring, nor at the window. Between her mother and mine there was little love lost.

When I met her we were not alone by ourselves. We were eight hard-working lads, determined to learn what it was to conjugate a verb, and to bring civilisation into our village. And five or six girls used to come for two hours a day, and sit on the other side of our old schoolmaster, and did their parsing with such grace, that willy nilly, you must needs fall in love with grammar.

This grace came, of course, because they were all little ones, not that they were all pretty—to my taste, pretty was only one, and she was my beloved !

What have I said ? Since when my beloved, and how long ? I had never said a word to her. Never with so much as a finger had I touched her plump little hand. No breath of mine could come nigh to caress her. The only thing that passed from my lips to hers was the word " I love," as we conjugated it tense by tense in turn, and it so fell out that I was last in our row and she was first of the little girls. " We had been loved, you had been loved," she began to repeat, then stumbled and smiled, while I, who had been watching day after day for a chance of giving her a smile, even though it might be only half a one, beamed all over my face as I looked upon her, with no fear that the master might spy out our dangerous secret. Down fell her eyes upon her book, red blushed her two cheeks, and the girl beside her began the next tense.

Eyes, and once more eyes ! Without you, neither first love nor last love could we have had. My looks as she came in to the lesson, her looks as she left to go home, these were our vows, our love-songs, our kisses, these were the only love-letters for us. In course of time, without a word said between us, we elaborated this language of the eyes until it became a science. Our glances were of all sorts and kinds. There was the indifferent glance, that pierced me to the heart ; the angry glance, that seared me as with a flash of lightning. There was the treacherous look given to another, that melted me like wax and destroyed me utterly. Then again would come the gentle and sweet look

of love, that uplifted my soul again into its place,
and I was at peace. My own glances, expressive
though they were, had none of these terrible
changes: there was the same devotion, the same
grief, the same mute agony in them all.

Three months must have gone by thus. I woke
each morning at the first call, and was all impatience for school-time. My mother was proud of
me, and already looked upon me as a future
bishop.

I was always the very first at the school door,
and yet I never once had the luck to find her alone,
either on the way or on the spot. That was my
eager desire, that was my dream: to see her alone,
were it for one moment only; to tell her once for
all that I was dying, that I was undone, that other
hope for my life was there none unless I could have
her love for ever. All this I said with my burning eyes, but my unsatisfied heart longed for
speech; it knew not measure nor reason, but cried
to me continually—" Forward! love has other joys
than these!"

But how to make her understand that I wanted
speech of her? Looks were not enough for that;
there must be a letter. A thousand times I wrote
and re-wrote that letter. I carried it with me,
resolved not to let my shyness overmaster me, not

to fear either master or top boy, only to give her
the paper secretly in a book, an inkstand, anything
that came handy. The hour came, my heart
shrank! I durst not! And I carried the paper
home again, and tore it to shreds, and cursed the
day that I was born to be such a useless coward.

Summer was just beginning when I got up one
morning, and went to the shrine of the Holy
Virgin, and made a vow that I would that day give
her my letter; and if I did not, I prayed fire might
descend and consume me.

That day I was the first at school again. All
the boys and girls came in. My eyes were dim
with looking towards the door; in vain—my little
girl was not there. The master called the roll;
when he came to the name of Argyró, there was no
answer.

" Where's Argyro ? " asked the master of one of
her little friends.

" Her mother's ill, and she stayed at home."

A heavy heart I had within me as I went home
that midday ! What could I do, and where could
I go, till evening should pass and day should dawn
once more !

Day came, and I went to school; it was the
same as before. A week went by ; a fortnight ; a
month had passed, when one morning a girl told

the master that Argyro's mother was dead, and the little girl was not coming back to school.

I was somewhere about five-and-twenty when I made my first visit home after my travels. All my old friends, lads and lasses, came to see me. And from the other end of the village came Argyro, now a matron with two children. Then I spoke to her, and she to me, for the first time. We told each other a thousand things ; spoke of her children, how pretty and clever they were ; about my travels, and how glad I was to find my old mother so well. On all these matters our talk ran like a river ; and about that first love of ours, that love never forgotten, as of old, so now, we said not a single word.

ANGELICA

GREAT was the excitement when our village first saw Angelica. People accustomed to the shy and demure village maidens, suddenly saw in their midst a woman who seemed to them a kind of goddess. In the first place, she was snow-white, as if the sun had never seen her; secondly, she was merry, laughing, lively, drove them all out of their senses when she laughed and showed her fine teeth; thirdly, she wore no country garb, but all her dresses came from town. But why speak of firstly, secondly, or tenthly? Such she was that when you looked at her you could not look enough.

A complete revolution was made in the village by Angelica. The worthy villagers did not reckon upon this bad result; their aim was quite innocent. They were on the look-out for a good school-mistress, to teach the girls their letters. So they wrote to town, and in a little while down came Angelica.

There was no proper school building as yet. She was given the use of a cottage, and in that cottage Angelica began to civilise the little village girls. So far so good ; the little girls learnt that in books we do not eat bread, but call it by some fine book-name[1] ; and when they had finished their lessons they began to sew. Then in the evening, when they came home again, they showed their fathers what they had been doing; some hemming, a pair of slippers, or an embroidered tobacco-pouch. And the fathers looked at these, and were proud to think that at last the girls had seen something of refinement.

But things did not stop here. The big girls, who could no longer go to school, must not be left in the lurch. It would be a shame if their younger sisters went out into the world better and more polished than they ! So they made a dead set at Angelica, and left her no peace. Not a party gathered of an evening, but she was among them, telling stories, describing town customs, singing the town songs, chatting and gossiping, while they forgot all the village games, songs, and stories, and sat as if bewitched, listening to Angelica.

It is true that when the school-mistress went to her cottage, the village girls (this was an art they could never forget) made a thousand jokes at the poor creature's expense. One would mimic her

---

[1] An attempt is being made in Greece to resuscitate classical words where they have fallen out of use.

voice, another her unfamiliar words, another her roguish looks. Innocent jests they were, with no envy in them and no malice, only made for a piece of fun. And even as they burst out laughing, they would begin again to admire her red lips, her white teeth, her little feet, her gait, her dresses and gewgaws, all her gracefulness and her beauty.

And by sheer force of gazing and admiring, the village girls began gradually to change their ways. This change was certainly slow, and only on the surface; her nature no village maiden can ever change. So they altered a few of their words, some of their manners, some of their clothes and ornaments. It was just this that made the village folk look with a less favourable eye on the luxurious witch who had done it. They were no longer content with home-spun stuffs and silks; they must go to the shop for all manner of ribbons, buttons, and rags. And the worst of it was that the imitation could not be complete; and you would suddenly see bonnet and gaudy necklaces together, or French furbelows worn along with their short fur jacket, and so forth. The fathers, of course, took no notice of this. Perhaps in their hearts they were proud of it. What troubled them was that it touched their pocket; new expenses were the revolution which the master of the house saw and dreaded.

And the more the daughter adorned herself, the more care the father took of his own greasy coat or patched shoon.

Nor was even this the end. Angelica, as we have said, was lively and fond of talking. So by degrees the village maidens found their tongues wag looser, even in presence of a stranger. Perhaps one or another would even be pert to her own father. The most prominent men of the village loved their village, and wished for its improvement. But they loved their home even more, and ever as they sat in the coffee-house, running their beads through their fingers, they were thinking how to put some check upon that school - mistress. To drive her away would not do ; some school-mistress they must have. Who knows but they might find a worse ?

" I have it ! " cried one of them one day—Spanós, they called him, the Beardless, though he certainly had a beard. " We must marry the woman. Let her get a home of her own, and live and let live."

" How can you marry her ? Didn't you hear her say the other evening to my daughter, that it was a shame that she should allow herself to be mated by her parents, instead of choosing her own mate ? "

" Ah ! well, then, we must let her choose the man herself. A little skill, and the thing is done."

By good luck it happened that there was in the village a certain gay dog, a headstrong fellow, the master builder, Myzíthras.[1] One evening Spanos went to the tavern, made straight for Myzithras, and with a few words hatched the plot.

" Why do you sit there, your youth and good looks going to waste?" said he to the man. " Where can you find such a Nereid, such a fleck of sea-foam, such a lily? What do you want prettier than such a woman as this? You have something of your own; what does it matter if she has no dower to bring? Off with you, and get up a serenade for her. If you're afraid of a serenade, then a flower, an excuse, and the thing's done! Why waste words about it? Go to her house this evening to see whether the new wall is sinking. Say I sent you. Don't be afraid. You make a beginning; and as for the end, never mind about that—I am here."

Myzithras at first took all this for some little joke on the part of our friend Spanos. He knew how fond Spanos was of teasing, and paid little heed. Still, on his way home that evening, Myzithras did not sing as his use was. He was plunged in strange thoughts; he had no peace.

---

[1] The word means cream cheese.

Why should Spanos try such a joke on him? Why should it not be truth? What harm to try? If he succeeded, what man in all the village would have such a treasure for his wife? If he failed, and it got about, and they made a song about her, let Spanos look out; he should smart for it.

Up the hill he came, and stopped one minute before the school to take breath. One glance he cast at Angelica's windows, and he had an impulse to strike up a song, like fury. However, he refrained and went forward. He reached the door. Now his heart was trembling, his throat was dry, a fine sweat broke out upon his skin. He stooped down, and peeped through the keyhole before knocking. In the middle of the yard stood the maid; but the door of the room was open, and inside was Angelica, sitting by a little table, and working embroidery.

"Spanos was quite right," said he, "a Nereid she is, the little devil! Well, what am I to begin with when I get in? Eh, I'll just say good evening, and God will manage the rest."

He knocked at the door. The maid opened it, and in walked our master workman.

Angelica rose, half frightened. She stood by the lamp, with her black eyes wide open, as who should ask what he might want at such an hour.

"Good evening to you, and a candle, please,"
says he; "I want to give a look at the cellar, as
the new wall is sinking, they tell me, and Master
Spanos has sent me to see."

"Maroúla!" cried Angelica, "light a candle and
give it to the builder; he wants to look round.—I
hope there's nothing wrong."

"I looked at it carefully from outside, and saw
nothing. All the same, we'll have a look from
within."

Down he went into the cellar, and after a while
came up to say that there was no danger with the
wall, but she had better say nothing about it, or
people might be afraid to send their children to
school.

Thereupon Myzithras stood still a moment in
front of her. Now Myzithras was by no means
uncomely. Tall he was, with big brown eyes and a
small military moustache, and he had a pleasant
address. But you see this time his tongue was
tied. What could he find to say, and the maid
within hearing too!

"Let's take a look inside the school," says he,
suddenly, scanning the walls.

And he took the light, and went by himself into
the schoolroom, wondering how he was to begin his
conversation.

"See here!" cried he to her from the school-room.

Angelica hastened in.

There was a dim flicker of light from the candle in that great room. Angelica stepped lightly up until she stood before him, like a statue, with her negligé dress, her black eyes, her white neck, and her two little hands pressed together on her bosom as if she felt rather cold.

"Master Spanos must have seen this crack, and been alarmed. A little mortar is all that it wants. The house is sound, and it has turned out a lucky one too. All our girls are civilised within its walls."

"Very nice of you to say that!" laughed Angelica.

"My dear lady, we country folk call things by simple names. I would tell you another piece of truth, if I were not afraid you might take it ill."

"What is that?" asked Angelica, moving a step nearer.

"That there is one soul in the village who is over head and ears in love with you."

"Goodness, what do you mean? and what soul is it, if you will be so good as to tell me? Tell me now where nobody can hear us."

" And if you are angry ? "

" I vow I won't be angry, whoever it may be. Why should I be angry ? "

" All right, you shall hear the rest. There is a certain man, who is neither old, nor poor. He is not a very good scholar, but he has seen something of the world in his time ; he learnt his trade abroad. A skilled workman is what he is. He does not know how to tell his trouble like a book, but he can sing it like a bird in the bushes. He can't say how d'ye do in French, but he knows how to love and fondle in his native Greek."

" And his name ? " asked Angelica, stamping her foot.

" I can't tell you his name, I dare not." And here Myzithras stopped short.

" Not though he is tall, nice, a fine young fellow, and pleasant-spoken ? " asked Angelica again, laughing.

" I can't tell you, I can't. My mind is going out like this candle." And he put the candle on a bench, and looked down thoughtfully.

" What's the matter, lad ? what's up with the poor fellow ? "

Then Myzithras turned round, looked straight at her and said—

> " Nothing works such deadly ill,
> Nothing does so surely kill,
> As when a secret lover
> His hurt dare not discover."

The schoolmistress perhaps had some suspicion, and still wished to play him for the fun of it, perhaps she really wished to hear some more ; be it how it may, she put on an innocent air, and said—

" You are in love, I can see. And who is that unhappy lady-love, who does not know the trouble you are in ? "

This time Myzithras gave her a burning glance, and murmured,

> " Angelica is sugar sweet, and honey to my thinking ;
> A fresh, cool spring, whence angels bring the water for their
>   drinking."

Angelica could not pretend not to understand this. A shiver ran through her. It really was not prudent to stay with this man. He might dare to stoop down and kiss her ! So she withdrew a step or two, put on her usual air at meeting a stranger, and said,

" Well, so there's nothing wrong with the wall. Many thanks for your trouble." And in she went.

Myzithras was half dazed. He was under the lash of love and shame. He looked round for some means of getting out, which would not bring him near the haughty Angelica. Spying the door by which the little girls came in at schooltime, he opened it and straight out, without letting even a footstep be heard.

As he left the courtyard and descended the hill, and felt the air upon his brow, he recovered himself and his shame passed off, but the love remained still. And when he came yet further down, and saw the open country before him, and the moonlight playing on the sea, the inspiration awoke in his heart, and he sang for all the world to hear—

"I bid good-night to one sweet soul, whose name I keep unspoken ;
For if I try the name to cry, with tears my voice is broken."

.   .   .   .   .   .

" Some more, please, some more of those wonderful ditties of yours," said Angelica one evening to the girls, as they sat, a happy party, with darning or embroidery around the light. "They are sweet, so sweet and pretty, they have the scent of basil in them; sing me some more, I am dying for these country flowerets which you despise, you poor creatures, and don't know what a treasure is yours! Oh, village life for ever! When could we spend such an evening as this in town? Where could we hear such songs, sweet as musk! Let me learn them,

let me learn your songs too.   I can't live without
them !"

And she began at once to sing to a village air :—

" My tall and slender cypress tree, stoop down and listen to
    me ;
    A word or two I fain would say ; and then let death pursue
    me ! "

A ripple of laughter ran round the group of
girls.

" How prettily she sings, as if she had been born
in the place ! "

" Pooh ! where do you suppose I was born ?   In
a village, to be sure, and they carried me off to
town when I was ever so small, and had neither
mother nor father.   My poor old uncle took me
to town and brought me up.   I remember my poor
mother as if it were yesterday.   There ! that's what
she was like.   Everybody said I was the image of
her."

And she took a kerchief, and bound it about her
head, and looked at them with a quiet and thoughtful glance.   She was a real picture then.

The girls sat gazing at her, silent and much
moved ; two or three actually felt tears in their
eyes.

" You are one of us, Angelica ! " says one, the

eldest ; "only don't imagine that you can turn us
into Frenchwomen ! "

"I turn you into Frenchwomen ?   God forbid !
Take care you don't make me one, now that I have
been changed back again into a village maiden.
Another week, and you'll have to sing the bridal
song for me ! "

They were thunderstruck.   Down dropt their
sewing upon the ground, they looked at each
other, they began to titter violently, leapt upon
their feet, clustering round Angelica to hear what's
in the wind.

"Let me alone, and I'll tell you.   Pooh ! it's
simple enough.   I'm in love with a young man,
and I'm going to have him.   Don't be jealous.
He's not engaged to any one else.   He belongs
to the other side of the village.   He is not
old, he is not poor.   He's not a very good
scholar, but he knows his business.   He can't
tell me his love like a book, but he can sing
like a bird in the bushes."

"And his name ? " they all cried.

"His name ? something that is nice with honey."

"*Myzithras!* cream cheese !" called out the eldest.

"Very well, you who guessed it shall be a
bridesmaid, and help to adorn the bride.   The
marriage takes place from Master Spanos' house."

And so it happened. Spanos took the whole affair on himself, as if he had been her father.

As for Angelica, she became a regular village bride. The gold tassels were there, and all the thousand and one ornaments and trickeries that make the country folk call a wedding by the name of " rejoicing."

And as for the bridegroom, his joy knew no bounds. Even during the " crowning " of the pair, he stepped aside and whispered to our good friend Spanos—

" I am a king, Angelica is my crown, and you are my ' Grand Vizier ! ' "

And he said the truth. Like a true Grand Vizier Spanos had managed the whole business. He it was who, after that evening, went and fanned the flame in Angelica's heart. He it was arranged the match with Myzithras' mother ; and within the fortnight all was ready, and the good dame settled down with her son and his bride, and resolved to live with them, to take care (as she said) of her grandchildren when Angelica was at school.

And so the schoolmistress became mistress of a house, dressed and spoke and behaved like the rest of the world, and saved the village girls from their craze when they wanted to become so many Frenchwomen.

OLD THANOS

HE was an old man, it's true; but his heart grew never old. He worked like a lad, thought like a man, loved like a mother. Love cherished the whole life of him. As a young man he worshipt his darling Maro—Maro who stayed with him hardly long enough to give him one dear and only girl. When he followed her to the grave his hair showed a patch of grey; one terrible night had sprinkled white on those grizzly locks, the night when Maro gave birth to little Phróso, when Thanos went into her room and suddenly saw a dear little baby girl by the side of its dead mother.

As he grew older Thanos loved Phroso, his only child. For her he lived, for her he worked in his tiny garden. But for her how could he have borne the loss of his beloved Maro?

Time must either heal a sorrow or bury it as in a tomb, be it of the body or of the soul. Those sixteen years, which you could see blooming in Phroso's maiden face, had healed his sorrow for Thanos. Only now and again he felt some hidden depth stir within him as he looked upon her. The little girl was the image of her dead mother.

Even this secret pain was lost when Phroso was married. He shed tears, it is true ; but tears of joy.

Ah ! if Charon had only taken away this second love of his !—alas—it was not Charon this time, it was the devil. When Thanos had a grandchild born to him, when he planted a third love in his heart, pretty Phroso went wrong and ran away, her husband went mad with despair, and the old man was left all alone in his cottage with a baby Maro.

Now his hair went white all over ; and now his lips trembled, and his heart bled with two grievous wounds. The wound that Phroso had dealt opened again the old wound of his first love. If only his good Maro had lived, thought he, this terrible thunderbolt would never have fallen upon his house.

There were times when he broke down utterly. He would take the little one upon his knees, and watch her as she laughed and tried to catch hold of his beard ; and this was too much for him ; his heart was nigh breaking. He would put the little one down on the ground, and out again into the garden to dig, and dig, and dig. The sweat ran from every pore ; he gave himself no rest. He would come in again worn out and exhausted. He ate with a good appetite, and then slept like lead.

"How can the man have such an appetite and sleep like that?" some of the neighbours wished to know. "God must have given him those blessings for the sake of his little Maro."

Yes, the god whose name is Hard Work.

UNCLE ANASTASIS

" BUT for that poor fellow we should be worse off
than we are."

These words were said to me one evening by good
Master Asímis, the headman of the village whither
I had come, a couple of months before, to treat the
sick there in my capacity as physician. They were
caused by the sight of a man some sixty years of
age, with a long fez and thick girdle, a stick in one
hand and a string of beads in the other, with bushy
gray eyebrows, a firm-closed mouth, and a look of
determination.

"How so ? " I asked ; " who is he ? "

" It's Uncle Anastásis.   Did you never hear the
name ? "

I felt somewhat embarrassed.   Still, I had not
been in the village long, and Master Asimis for-
gave me for not knowing who Uncle Anastasis was.

" But for that good fellow, we should not have a
drop of water in the place."

And he began to explain how Uncle Anastasis
had set to and made the people bring water into

the village, from a distance of five or six miles;
how much money he had contributed, and how
much trouble he had taken to make others give;
what a concourse there had been when the water
ran from the first duct, where nobody knew what
running water was like, except in the spouts which
filled the cisterns in the large houses.

And he sat down, with me near him, and went
on to describe what happened each evening in the
houses that had cisterns, where everybody used to go
and draw water or refresh themselves.

"They couldn't rest till it was evening, and time
for the girls to go to the courtyard, pitcher in hand.
They used to put their pitchers by, and forget their
thirst for a while, to gossip. After chatting together an hour or so, they began to wind the winch.
And then they drank, and called blessings on the
dead of that family. And then some giddy wench
would give a shove to another, and the other would
douse her with water, and chase her right out into
the road; all the rest screeching with laughter."

"But what has all that to do with Uncle Anastasis, who passed by just now?"

"I'm coming to that. He was young once, like
the rest of us, and as you are now, sir. He had a
wife, and he had a little boy three years old. All
his life and joy was in them. His house you see

yonder by the big sycamines; that's his garden.
There's a spring there too, but the water is brack-
ish. The good water was in his well, in the middle
of the courtyard. In winter he had it full to the
brim. As summer went on, the water got lower
and lower, and the well rang to the smallest tap on
its metal cover. This echo used to amuse the child.
He would run and strike the cover, and then look
at his mother and laugh. Next he wanted to see
inside. So the mother held him, and let him peep
in, and the youngster saw the other little child who
was reflected at the bottom in a circle of light.
This game was played many a time. It happened
once that the child was livelier than usual, and the
mother less careful. As the child gazed at the little
face in the water, it came into his head to knock
with his hand upon the winch, with the rope of the
bucket wound round it, to see if there would be an
echo. The baby slipt from his mother's hands, and
got entangled in the rope; round went the winch,
down went the rope, and the baby was in the water!
While the mother stooped to catch her child, she
got to one side, and as the winch went round like
mad, its iron handle struck her head, and left the
poor creature lifeless!"

"Enough, enough, thank you. I'm a doctor,

true, but I don't come here for such stories as
that."

"A good thing if it were nothing more than a
story! Only if it had been a story, we should have
no water in the village to-day. All his widowed
years were passed by the poor fellow crying for
water! Running water! They must close in the
wells, and make an end of the dreadful echo. And
he had his way. He brought us to our senses,
and now we have a great blessing on the place."

"A great blessing out of a great evil," said I to
Master Asímis.

THE BOAT

" WHY do you stand gazing in this meditative way at yonder boat ? " asked Marie one evening of Phótis, her husband, as they sat together near the window, down by the sea-shore.

" Oh, I'm looking at the sea, and wondering at its beauty. What else should it be ? "

" No, you weren't looking at the sea ; you were looking at the boat. What boat is it ? "

" All right, I was looking at the boat with its white sails."

" And what were you thinking of ? "

" What luck it might bring for us ! "

" Christ and Our Lady ! He might at least have the civility to answer a civil question ! " And out went Marie, in a pet.

Photis remained alone. He cast one glance at the door, smiling, lifted his head, and began talking to himself.

" I saw, I saw,—what's the use of telling you what I saw, my good Marie ? Your fate and mine is what I saw. My love and my hope, that's what I saw ! "

And Photis turned again to the sea, and gazed at the little ship.

"There you are, anchored again. Down with the sails, let go the anchor. Out go the sailors, and straight away to the tavern. Out roll the barrels and their bad smells. There are our sweet hopes. Go down to look at them, and to enjoy them : salted sardines is what you find, and the smell of bilge-water."

And he stopt again, meditating.

"It's three years agone since I saw a boat, a long, long way off, on the edge of the horizon. A white speck, nothing more. But how beautiful it looked upon the blue sea! I gazed at it, and could not gaze enough. Slowly, slowly the speck became a sail, all complete, and a fine sail it was in that unforgotten bark. And what a butterfly the boat was! A thing of fairyland! A year went by, and still the little ship was skimming over the blue sea. Yet another year and you could see its graceful hull as it cut through the waves that came rolling on, ever rolling. Soon you could descry the sailor in the boat; what an enchanting sight! a very god he seemed sailing in her. You would have said the bark was playing with the waves as it drew near the shore. You could hardly help going to embrace it, as if it had been a thing alive. Now you could hear the soft ripple of the water as it foamed away from her flying prow; you could hear the sail flapping in the breeze as it came down. Down came the sail; up rose the sailor and folded it, took the pole and pushed her ashore. I ran down to greet the little bark. And what a sight it was then! Insufferable! Bilge-water and fish, old planks and tarry ropes, lying here and there! And the sailor—a worn-out wizened creature, with never a good-evening for me! Ah, that was my love and my hope! A white-winged yacht in the distance, and, when it came to anchor, a fishing smack full of filthy bilge-water!"

PARASKEVAS AND HIS DAUGHTER

PARASKEVÁS was a widowed labourer, with one little girl, and an old mother. I know his house well. You enter his courtyard, and darkness over-shadows your soul ; day cannot enter there. You grope your way to the right hand corner, and there you find the door of his kitchen. We will call it kitchen, because there he cooks his food and eats it too ; but they sleep there in winter time, because it is warmer.

A first-rate worker, and a tender-hearted father was Paraskevas. At dawn he used to rise, and before going out into the fields, he took his little girl, danced her up and down in the air, and rub-bing his rough moustache on her cheeks, kissed her again and again. Then he used to take his basket and out to his work.

In the evening when he returned, there were other scenes. He never came home straight. Unhappily, Paraskevas was fond of his glass. He would drop in at the tavern, and there quaff away merrily. At home the old dame sat with the child,

and sang to her or told stories. Until three o'clock
or so (Turkish time [1]) she would sometimes sit
waiting. Then the little one grew drowsy, cuddled
up to its grandam, and went to sleep. The old
woman would spin, with now and again a sigh.
Then her son would come home, blind drunk.
The old dame used to carry out the light to keep
him from stumbling in the darkness, and lead him
in. Then there was scolding and complaining.
Everything went wrong; nothing satisfied him.
His mother listened and bore it all; was she not
his mother?

However, there was one thing our hero never
forgot. The child was by this time lying asleep
on her little bed; and the father used to go and lift
up the coverlet and look lovingly at her with his
drunken eyes. " Bless you, sweetheart ! " he always
murmured, in his hoarse voice. The child would
turn over on her side, perhaps annoyed by the
fumes of the drink from her father's breath.

Then they sat down to supper, and soon sleep
carried them all to a more peaceful world.

It happened one evening that the old woman was
out, having been called to a neighbouring house, to
help at a birth. She had put the little girl to bed,
and hung the light outside the door of the kitchen,

---

[1] *i.e.*, three hours after sunset.

that her son might see his way in; and went to
her neighbour's house to lend her aid to the poor
woman. She sent word to Paraskevas at the tavern
that he might know.

Paraskevas returned at the usual time. He
opened the outer gate and went in as usual, rolling
drunk; it was all he could do to keep his feet.
He took down the light from above the door, and
entered the kitchen, staggering this way and that,
leaning against the wall with one hand, and with
the other holding the light, which he waved to and
fro in the air like a censer.

What happened exactly when he came in nobody
ever could find out; but it seems that he stumbled
over something and fell, dropping the lamp right
upon his little girl's bed. He shouted like a madman; then he fell silent, and the child began to
shriek. He must have spilt all the oil over the
bed; for when the old dame (who had heard the
noise) arrived on the spot, the coverlet was one
mass of fire.

"God help us!" cried the old woman, as she
ran up, seized the carpet which was stretched out
in the corner, and threw it upon the bed. The
flames were put out, and the child was silent. A
terrible silence that! When she took off the
carpet, the child was unrecognisable; her face

was charred, and red rims of blood about her eyes.

It was my lot, being a doctor, to see this awful sight. When they called me in, Paraskevas sat weeping like a little child.

Months and months I visited that house. The child's life was saved; she is now about thirteen years old. The marks of burning will remain always on her face; but its sweetness could not be burnt out of it. The poor little thing lives alone, for her grandmother departed this life soon after. But her evenings are now passed in her father's company; for, after that terrible evening, never again did Paraskevas enter a tavern.

SECRET LOVE

" Is it true, doctor, that in sickness a man sometimes is delirious, and tells secrets in his delirium ? "

" Well, look here," said I to my friend. " I have
more often heard the truth from the sick and crazy,
than from anybody else, when they are well. You
shall hear what happened to me in the case of a
girl of that village yonder, some little time ago.

" She was ill for six days. One evening she was
in a strong fever, and they hastened to bring me
word. No one else was present except her mother,
a quiet woman and somewhat narrow-minded. The
poor soul was crying, and begged me to save her
girl. I did what I could, and stayed a little while
in the house to see what course the fever would
take. I went up to see her again ; she was worse,
unconscious, and her mind wandering. From her
talk it seemed she saw flowers and thorns. She
touched a flower, and she turned to smile at you.
Suddenly a thorn pricked her—you could see the
pain in her face. Play of fancy, said I to myself.
But with one of the flowers that her wandering

mind was gathering, she turned her face round, as
before, and murmured 'loves me, loves me not,'
quite low, and incoherently, twitching her fingers
as though she pulled off the petals one by
one.

"A word to the mother, and we went downstairs
to wait a little longer. When we got down, the
mother sat by the cooking-stove to make me a cup
of coffee. And as she made it, she talked and
talked of her girl, what an angel she was, a girl of
gold, such a housekeeper! and she spoke the truth.

"'But tell me,' I asked her then, 'has your
daughter ever had a lover?'

"'God forbid, my dear doctor! Never was a
more innocent lamb than my darling Lenió, God
save her!'

"The good woman thought that a girl must be
a brazen hussy to be in love. That's what she
learnt of love in her school.

"'But think,' said I, 'hasn't the girl some
secret sorrow? Perhaps it will be easier to cure
her, if we know.'

"'Sick as she is, doctor, I had rather see her in
her grave than that she should stain our honourable
name!'

"I saw that my words were thrown away; so I
drank my coffee, took another look at the patient,

gave some medicine for the night, and took my leave.

"Three days afterwards, the girl died. I do not say she was not ill, but the girl's nerves were a wreck, and a little happiness, a caress, might have saved her.

"I went to the funeral, for I pitied the poor thing. It broke my heart to see the mother tearing her hair over the body, adorned for burial, in which nothing of life was left but a peaceful smile.

"The moment came for that hymn which calls us to take our last kiss of the dead. Scarce had they drawn away the inconsolable mother from the girl's cold face, when there came near a lad of eighteen or so, wishing to offer a last kiss with the rest. He came from the neighbourhood, and was acquainted with the family; I think he and the girl had been at school together. So it was no wonder that he too should come up with tears in his eyes. They lifted the body, laid it in the grave, the people dispersed, and I prepared to leave also. But instead of going out by the great door, I wanted to get to the postern leading into the upper path, so as to come by the market-place; and thus I made a circuit behind the church. Just outside the Sanctuary, in a lonely corner, what should I see but that very lad who kissed the face

of Lenio.   He was weeping hot tears, poor fellow.
I thought for a moment that I would go up and
speak to him, and say what Lenio had done in her
fever.   But my heart could not bear it.   His love
had been born in secret; and in secret it should
die."

FIRE

It was about midnight. A boy of twelve years, Stephanákis, was sleeping like a lamb, when suddenly his mother came to him, and awoke him with a good shake. The boy half rose, rubbed his big eyes; and what was that he saw through the opening of the window! A great and terrible fire! They got him up, put on his clothes, and led him outside.

"Down to his uncle's house," said the mother to the maid, who had charge of him; "and let him get to sleep quickly, or else he'll be ill."

They stood still a moment in the garden which divided their house from the house that was burning, and looked at the fire. A terrible sight it was. Huge tongues of flame darted up from the pit that was once a roof, as though trying to devour the sky. At a house near by, a man was standing at a window, and throwing into the road tables, chairs, and bedding. The cries of the neighbours well-nigh deafened you. The father of Stephanakis, on the top of his house opposite the fire, was running about, crying for help, throwing buckets of water upon the carpets that hung from his roof, trying to defend his own house, which the greedy flames licked here and there at every gust of wind. All this little Stephanakis saw, and trembled with fear. At last the maid caught him by the hand, and as she was setting out in the direction of his uncle's house, the mother ran up behind them, bidding them wait for Aspasia. Aspasia was the daughter of the man who was throwing his chairs and tables out of the window: a little girl, and an only child.

They took their way down, and arrived at their destination. As soon as they got inside, they hurried to the window to see a sight which they never could forget. The window looked in the direction opposite to the fire. They saw the sea and the hills beyond it, all illuminated. You might have thought that the day had already dawned, but for the stars.

The little lad was not very much discomposed; he rather enjoyed this unusual occurrence. But as for the girl, she was quite upset, and her heart bled. It was for a doll that her heart bled; she had lost it in some dark corner. What would become of poor dolly if their house should take fire, and who would save her? The child began to cry, and the boy could not get to sleep again; the girl's crying made him sorry.

All the others went to sleep. The boy got up, and said to his little neighbour: "I'll go and get your doll." And out he went, very quietly. By this time the fire had been got in hand; still it had not ceased to burn, and before long Stephanakis was close to the little girl's house, and there he stood in front of it, in the midst of all their goods and chattels.

"Aspasia's doll!" he said.

The girl's father turned round, and saw the boy with alarm.

"What do you want here?" said he.

The lad again asked for the doll.

"Here, take it, and be off, you imp, before your parents see you," said he, and pulled out of his pocket a home-made doll, with eyes, nose, and mouth, all drawn in ink, upon a lump of calico tied into a knot to make its face.

The child took the doll, and fled.

When she saw it, the little girl's face beamed with joy. She hugged her dolly, and went to sleep.

And now, how shall I explain it? Was it because of the doll's story? or was it some other reason? Anyhow, as a matter of fact, Stephanakis and Aspasia are now man and wife.

THE BURIED TREASURE

" SUCH a fine man, and dead in five days ! "

" And such a regular life, too ! "

" These strong men, it seems, fall at one blow, and then they seldom rise again."

" Tell us, doctor, and a blessing on your eyes, what made our good schoolmaster die so suddenly?"

I could not get rid of them : I had to tell the story. Well, it did not much matter. So I lit my cigarette, called for coffee, and began :

" It is now six days since the evening when we had him among us. You remember how he strode in, fresh and ruddy with walking. You remember his jokes and laughter. A good fellow he was, true gold, God rest him. He went home that evening, quite early, as he always did. It so happened that I went with him. We sat in the verandah ; his cousin joined us, the master of the Parish School ; and being two schoolmasters and a doctor together, of course we talked about books, learning, and such-like. The odd thing was that we got on the subject of religion, and from religion we passed to

superstition and popular beliefs. The good fellow
who now lies dead had no patience with superstition ; you know how stern he was about it. It was
late before we separated. In twenty-four hours he
was lying upon his bed, and I went to see him, and
found he had a severe chill. I prescribed for him,
and as I left, I asked his wife how he managed to
take that chill. She stood on the threshold outside the door, and said—

" ' I am ashamed to tell you, doctor, but I must.
I don't know what came over him last night; he
began to talk in his sleep, and frightened me by
what he said. I pulled his arm, and awoke him.
When he became conscious, he told me such a
strange dream. To tell the truth, I did not pay
much attention to what he said. I turned over,
and was half asleep again, when suddenly I heard
him get up. " Where are you going?" I asked.
" I can't help it," said he, " I must go downstairs.
If you want to know, wife, I'm going to do a mad
thing. If it succeeds, so much the better ; if not,
we lose nothing."

" ' I thought he must be losing his wits. I got
up, and tried to get him into bed again ; not a bit
of it. " I've seen it !" he cried. " I've seen it
clear as daylight in the earth, and I'm going to find
it and dig it up !"

" ' " What ? " I asked.

" ' " Ah, what! Well, I've seen in a dream that we have a treasure buried in the house. Near the big jar in the cellar."

" ' He struck a light, took the lamp, and down he went in his night clothes, just as he was. I went behind him. We got into the cellar, took pick and shovel, went to the corner by the big earthen jar, and stamping on the ground, cried out, " Here, I know it's here."

" ' What was I to do ? I began half to believe it myself. He dug, and I did the shovelling. Now and then, as he saw what a fool he was making of himself, he gave a laugh in the midst of his digging. Then I laughed too. We passed about two hours in this way. We dug down half a fathom or so ; not even a potsherd did we find ; nothing but solid, sifted earth. The cocks were beginning to crow.

" ' " That's enough," said I, " let's go back. That dream of yours did not visit you for good."

" ' He leant on his pick a moment, then said, " You're right. Let's fill up the hole again, and go to bed. It was a mad freak, and no mistake. You go up, and I'll follow soon."

" ' I went upstairs, and lay down in some distress. Before long he followed, bathed in sweat.'

"'Now I understand the business,' said I to her. 'Make him perspire as much as ever he can, to keep off pleurisy.'

"But all in vain.   Once Charon got his claws on that manly frame, there was no escape.   Each day he grew worse and worse.   On the last day, as I stood by his side, he turned and said to me : 'Doctor, haven't I shown what a good teacher I am ?   I teach one thing, and I practise——' and then he died."

IN THEIR DEATHS THEY WERE NOT DIVIDED

"Dear Doctor, a blessing on your eyes, tell me the truth. How is our patient inside there? I don't hear her moaning now. Tell me, in God's name! Is she alive, or is she ———"

"My good friend, where's your tongue running to?" said I to the sick man in the other room. "Your wife is alive and doing well. She has had no sleep for three nights, and she's sleeping now. Get a little sleep yourself; you are still feverish, and you must be quiet. I'm going to send you your sister, who has been looking after her bride all this time. Perhaps she is asleep too, after all this anxiety and watching."

And I left my patient, a young fellow newly married, to go into his wife's room, who had loved him, and had brought him to her own home from another village. A sudden sickness had laid them both low, and not a moment's time even to send word to her relations. The kind-hearted sister did everything, and even looked after the house as well.

I went into the other room, and in one glance saw what had happened. The sister was laying her hands upon the woman's eyes, and closing her mouth, and as I entered she turned and looked at me with her eyes full of tears.

I stooped to feel the pulse ; that too no longer beat, but had ceased along with her breath and her troubles.

" You want some woman to help you," said I to the sister. " Go and call some one, and I'll keep an eye on the patient till you return."

The girl threw a shawl over her head, and went out.

I remained alone in the house, with the sick man and the dead. I left the dead, and went into the sick man's room. I walked very quietly, so as not to awake the patient if he slept. He was half asleep when I entered ; a moment I stood watching his peaceful face, and hardly knew whether to be glad or sorry that there were signs of recovery upon that face, for all its weakness. Once he gets a good sleep, I thought, there's nothing to fear. But when he awakes from that sleep, what will the poor wretch see, and what will he hear ! I must have a word with the sister before she sees him, lest she let fall some word, or a tear, ere his strength comes back ; for if she does it is all up with him.

And very quietly I went out again, and descended the stairs, and went to the gate to watch for her coming. I had not long to wait; she returned with a woman, whose business it was to do that sad task of undressing and laying out, and then to watch the body.

"We must lay her bridal dress upon the poor thing," said she to the sister, as they stood by me at the gate.

I told them both as quickly as possible what they were to do, and how to behave, that the sick man might suspect nothing.

We went up quietly, all three together; I first, and the women behind me.

I entered the chamber of death — and there stretched on the ground was the husband, lifeless. I had no time to turn and tell the sister not to come in yet. I could only cover her face with my two hands, and say, "Go into your brother's room a moment."

The poor girl was alarmed, but did as she was bid. In coming out I made a sign to the woman that she must be silent, and let her in. I led the sister by the hand into the passage, and said to her:

"Before you go into your brother's room, I must tell you that he isn't there. You will find him side

by side with the wife he loved so well. In their
death they are not divided. He must have suspected the truth, and got up to see for himself.
Had he found her alive, he must have died, ill as
he was ; it is better that he found her dead, for his
death would have killed her."

I remained one day up there at the village, and
was in time to follow their bodies to the grave.

VANGELIS AND HIS NEW YEAR'S CAKE

THE north wind was blowing pitilessly; a few snow-flakes fluttered like butterflies, till they rested upon the dry rocks, to melt there. Down below, the sea was covered with foam, and the sun in the west was red like a fiery ball, in a cleft which there parted the clouds. Vangélis was just coming up from the harbour, on his way home. "The eve of St Basil," said he, "and New Year's Day to-morrow; let's go home. Let us begin the year well; per-haps we shall not quarrel any more. Perhaps God will enlighten the blessed woman, and for once in a way she may spare me those cursed speeches of hers, that cut right to the heart. You'll say that I'm as bad as she; that I have never a good word for her; that I sputter like a match at the smallest excuse; that I insult the poor thing. The woman's not a bad sort. Bah! A light head and a spice of obstinacy—and the mischief's in it. Then she'll say it is *I* who should be cool, and not provoke *her*. At least, for the sake of my poor, dear Pipina, this

squabbling ought to come to an end. Most certainly
I will turn over a new leaf this very night; and if
she says anything, I'll just hold my tongue, and so
we shall have some quietness. If I do that two
or three times, I shall get into the way of it, and
so we shall be at peace now and evermore."

With such thoughts as these in his mind, Vangelis
arrived at his own house. It was darker now. He
entered, saw a good blaze in the fire-place, and on
the fire a baking-pan. Little Pipina in her own
corner was watching the cake as it slowly browned,
and on the other side her mother, Sosána, was
melting honey. Frozen as he was with the cold,
he came forward to the fire, and stretched out his
hands to warm them.

"Ah, it's the very devil outside to-night!"
said he, looking at the fire, and trying to look
pleasant: no easy matter, with his disagreeable
face. "You there, little one! How's the New
Year's cake? not done yet, eh?"

Little Pipina was a charming sight, as the fire
shone upon her happy little face. She sat and
watched the cake slowly browning, much as a
young mother who sees her child begin to crawl.
What longing there was in that look, and what
love! And every now and again she just touched
the top with her finger-tip, to see if it was burning.

"And what's the matter that you have come to us so early this evening?" asked Sosana, poking the fire to make it burn up.

"Ah, what's the matter, yes! It isn't New Year every day!"

And Vangelis looked away, one hand spread to the fire, the other in the child's hair, caressing it.

"Glory be to God, who heard me when I burnt the incense this evening! And I told Him all about our misfortune, how we squabble every day and every hour! as if we couldn't live in any other way!"

"Come, never mind that now, but set the table; we're starving."

And rather roughly he caught up the child upon his knees, to keep himself from getting angry, and saying something worse. The little girl turned, and looked at him thoughtfully.

"What's wrong with you, my Pipina?" said he.

"What's wrong! *you* know what's wrong!" muttered Sosana, snorting; and got up to go out of the kitchen.

"Get thee behind me, Satan!" muttered Vangelis.

"What did you say?" Sosana was back in a moment, and called out from the door. Vangelis put the child down, crying by this time, and frightened. He got up, and went towards the

door, yellow as sulphur.   He looked at her with
eyes wide open, and said :

"What did I say ? I said that you are always
the same, living or dying ; that's what I said !"

The little girl cried aloud, but who had eyes for
the little girl ? The woman looked the man in the
face, and the man looked at the woman, like two
wild beasts ready to fly at each other's throats.

Sosana was the first to shift her gaze. She made
the sign of the cross, and calling on the Holy Virgin
to give her patience, turned to go out.

The little girl gave one glance at the cake again.

At the same moment, before Sosana had well got
outside, Vangelis too turned towards the fire-place,
murmuring that it was not her fault but his, for
coming home so early, as if he did not know her.

Again the child grew uneasy. She saw her
mother going away ; she knew what it all
meant, and tried to be herself again, her eyes
fixed on the ground in despair ; for her sweet
dream would never be fulfilled, the cake in the
midst and laughter and happiness all around.

"If you repent coming home betimes once in a
way, there's the door, and there's the tavern !" So
spoke Sosana, all in a tremble, with bitterness on
her lips.

The little girl trembled too.

"Accursed thou and thrice accursed!" cried Vangelis, beside himself, "that thou'lt not give a good Christian time to breathe, even if he wishes to do right! Serpent, thy bite is poison!"

Sosana stood still beside him; she seemed sorry to have provoked him, and was considering what to say or to do to smooth him down. But what could smooth down Vangelis now? Without another word, and still more angry that his wife had softened, he gave a kick to the New Year's cake, and sent it spinning among the coals and ashes, hurried out, and turned his back upon the house.

Never was that black evening forgotten by Pipina, the unhappy girl who now minds our village church. Never did she forget the tears that she shed then, nor the deep grief that half killed her until she fell asleep. Only she tells the story sometimes when she is better, when she is not lying unconscious with a terrible disease which overcomes her at intervals, and has done so ever since she was quite a little child. The parents have eaten sour grapes, and the children's teeth are set on edge.

THE SHEPHERD BOY

THE spot where stood the lonely shrine of St Try-phonas was not a spot to go into raptures over. There was not a tree near it, no water, and no cultivated land. Thorns as many as you like up above, along the hillside ; but down by the sea-shore, round the barren walls of the lonely shrine, *agnus castus* bushes without end. That must be the place where the water from the hillside trickled down, hidden underground, and those bushes flourished exceedingly. After that you came to a delightful beach, covered with shingle, and beyond that the sea.

There was nothing unusual ; only bushes, hills, and sea. And yet, when all the village assembled here to do worship once in the year, how fair and delightful it was ! It was my wont to go down and stand at a little distance to watch that picture which I can never forget ; the thousand hues of our island costumes, inside the roofless enclosure, as many as could get in, and the rest all round. And I used to listen to their chants from afar, and I

could see the incense rising and spreading slowly
among the branches of the single tree that half
overshadowed the little chapel ; at least, let us call
it a tree : a wild olive, half withered, the other
half incessantly struggling for life, thanks to the
brine scattered over it by the north and north-east
gales—such was the tree you saw, just a little
higher than the bushes.   Near me I had other
music still,—the song of the larks.

The sun fell never upon that solitary nook till
the mass was over.   That sight, too, had a beauty
of its own ; to see for one whole hour the headlands
at either side of the little bay all golden, while you
did worship in the fresh cool of morning.

As I stood there, drinking in with all my eyes,
and with my whole being, those virginal beauties,
I espied a lad descending the hillside, and stopping
like myself at some little distance away to hear the
service. My eyes fixed themselves upon him without
any wish of mine.   He was drest as poorly as you
please, and he was bareheaded and barefoot. A short
pair of breeches left his feet and leg bare to the
knee ; but those finely modelled limbs, with the
soft down upon them, looking in the sunlight like
bronze, might in truth have been the envy of a
king's son.   So, too, his uncovered head, with its
clusters of fair curls, and his regular profile, fault-

less nose, the eyes full of life, the full lips. He
stood there like a statue, and in that pose, with his
round neck bent a little, he made me think of
those old figures which our great masters used to
carve, and I saw that the old stock is ever the
same.

I approached the boy,—I could not help it. I
asked him where he came from, who his father was.
He was the son of Widow Dexeropiá, from the
hamlet over the other side of the hill, and he watched
the goats of some proprietor, I forget who he was.
I gave him a halfpenny, which he took shyly, as he
talked shyly with me.

The congregation dispersed, and we went down
to the sea-shore. I joined my people ; we found a
place under a rock, gathered sticks and lit a fire ;
then we boiled some coffee, took out some of our
delicate biscuits, and broke our fast. Afterwards,
as we sat throwing pebbles into the sea, and talking, I said to one of my friends, who was some-
body in our own village—" I saw a lad this morning, on the ridge of that hill, whom you must get
away from his goats. It's a pity such a lad should
be lost on the hills. You'll find him a little shy,
but he is sharp ; take him, and you'll not repent
it. Send him to school for two or three years, and
then take him into the shop. He'll find his place."

My friend listened to me, and found a means of getting hold of the lad.

.   .   .   .   .

Many years afterwards, on my return from abroad, I remained a few hours in town to rest myself, and to find a good horse. As I sat in a friend's shop waiting, in came a fine young fellow, whose handsome build and pleasant look caused me surprise.

" I am that shepherd boy," said he, " whom you met at St Tryphonas' Chapel."

Though I had forgotten the story, it all came back to my mind at once, and I rose and embraced him as if he had been my own boy ; and, gripping his hand, I asked what brought him to town.

" I live here now," said he ; " and here I have been some five years. I came to better myself. Glory be to God, I have not failed. That shop opposite is mine. I import my calicoes straight from England."

" Ah ! and now you are rich, why won't you come with me to our village ? You see, I'm going there, poor as I am. Let's go together, and make your poor mother happy ! "

" Ah ! the poor dear is gone ! " said he, with a sad smile.

" Come, lad, to the place where your mother

sleeps, and leave this place before they *fix* you here," said I, seriously, and casting a glance upon him full of meaning.

" It is too late now," he answered. " I got married over here some time ago."

" All right, bring your wife with you, and come home and let other folks get rich. Remember our sweet home, my boy; remember that delightful hill, which you might turn into the hill of paradise ! You will find plenty and plenty to do there. Think of the gardens you can lay out, and the houses you can build ! "

" Oh, I see I must tell you all, to show you that it is impossible. Don't you think I long and crave for it myself ? But they won't hear of it, neither my wife nor her mother. They are grand folks ! They belong to the town. They wouldn't even go for a single day to see my humble village home. My wife doesn't care to hear about the place which knew me as a poor and sunburnt shepherd boy, as if it were not that hill that nursed this very heart of mine. . . ."

And there he stopt, for there was a lump in his throat, and his eyes were full of tears.

CHARON'S VICTIM

It was not quite an hour's walk from our house to the village where I saw Charon's Victim the other day for the first time. Her story I knew well. I knew her name, and her family. But it so happened that in my visits to that village I had never seen Charon's Victim with my own eyes.

It was a Saturday evening, and vespers had just ended. I stood one moment at the church door, and looked at the women coming out. Then I entered the church once more to light my taper before the shrine. When I had lit the taper, and prayed, I went into the porch, and looked out into the graveyard which lay beside the church. And there I saw a woman, all drest in black, who lit a taper over one of the graves, and wafted incense. Then she put down the censer before the taper, made the sign of the cross, and moved towards the gate, thoughtful, with downcast eyes, pale face, and on her lips a bitterness that suited as well with her looks now as the sweetness that they once must have had.

"That's our Charon's Victim," said the priest on duty. "What numbers and numbers of women suffer from the same incurable pain, and the name has clung to her out of them all! It is, a strange world. And so you will find in each village but one 'light-o'-love,' and one 'gossip,' and one acknowledged by all as the 'wise woman'."

.   .   .   .   .

And now that we have seen this poor adopted child of Charon's, let us tell her story in a few words.

She was an orphan girl, and eighteen years of age when her aunt found her a husband. The bride was pretty and good-tempered, the bridegroom a fine young fellow with a house of his own; what more could you wish? By-and-bye a little boy was born to them, and with his first smile the plant of their bliss broke into flower.

But no long time did the little angel stay with them. He took wing ere the year was out, and left them desolate. They would not be comforted. The mother reproached herself that she had left him now and then alone in his cradle while she went to the spring,—and would burst into weeping. And the father would reproach himself that once he frightened the babe to keep him quiet; and he too wept like a little child. They sat both together of an evening by the fireside, and all they said was about their darling.

A whole winter passed in this way. But when the next winter came, they had half forgot their little boy; and with the spring came a second child to them, a girl this time. There were the same rejoicings, the same caresses, perhaps the same scoldings when baby cried. But the pity of it, their luck was the same as before, and this poor little one stayed no longer than the last. So joy once more took wings and flew from their dwelling, and once more began weeping, and lamentation, and woe.

It might have been three months after they lost their baby, that Lampros's master (the great man of the place) ordered him to travel over to Roumelia to arrange some business for him, as he was being defrauded by his agents.

Another misfortune this! First death, then parting! Their hearts almost broke. Still they said, "Let us be patient; it is not for long." So Lampros left his wife in her aunt's charge, and departed.

The poor fellow did not know how he loved her until he had to part. He was broken-hearted over it all, and he had nothing to console him but his letters and hers, both full of longings and sighs.

"God be praised," she wrote to him once, "that it will not be long before I have my dear lad again."

And if she had only known! Lampros on his arrival found everything in confusion. He would have to stay at least one year to gather in the capital of his master's which had been scattered to the four winds. He tried to muster courage— "Courage!" came out of his heart with a sigh. And how could he write and tell her? It would kill her, poor thing; better to keep putting it off from day to day. It was but a year, and a year will have an end. Only he must write to her every week. And every week he wrote, and his wife answered with half-suppressed impatience, which would have become a hearty fit of passion if she could have spoken to him. Thanks to the master, who pitied them, one day she learned the truth, and he quieted her, and took her promise to be patient for a few months yet.

All months pass away, and so did these. It was a spring day, St George's Feast, and all the village was starting out for the feast. Her good neighbours pitied the poor woman, and did their best to persuade her to come along with them. Why not go out and enjoy herself a little? Lampros must find her well and strong, not pale as she

was then.   Her aunt said the same, and much
against her will, she went to join the throng.

    .   .   .   .   .

"Hurry up, Mitro, hurry up, let's get in before
dark; an hour more, and there we are!"

It was Lampros addressing his muleteer on the
evening of the feast of St George.   He had got
away from Roumelia a fortnight earlier than he
expected, perhaps wishing to give his wife a little
surprise.

He was almost beside himself as he rode over the
hills and through the woods.   He talked to himself,
he called out greetings, he laughed; he could see
her before him already, his beloved wife in their
peaceful home, sitting in a corner beside her aunt;
perhaps she was writing to him her last letter.

Another half hour, and they got up to St
George's.   There was a regular pandemonium over
there; all the field echoed with songs.

"See my luck!" said he to himself, "too late to
take the poor dear to the feast!   Never mind,
darling, we have the Feast of our Saviour, and then
you shall see!"

Scarce had the words left his lips when he met a
procession of men and girls returning to the village,
and singing as they went.   The sun had not quite
set, so he could still see them.   He knew them

all, and greeted them with a voice that trembled with his great joy. Before one fair form he was brought up short. Who could it be? How remarkably like his wife! As he looked at her thus, she heard her husband's name running from lip to lip, cried out—"My husband!" and fell swooning.

Lampros remained on his horse still as a stone, and could not find a word to say. A terrible thought, like a sword-thrust, ran through his mind. His wife at the feast, in a crowd of girls and men! And he had thought of her shut up in her home.

His mind could bear no more. He pulled the dagger from his belt, and at the moment when the women were trying to arouse the fainting woman to life, he fell to the ground, bathed in his own blood.

DIAMANTO

THE north wind that night had done its work well; and when day dawned, and Diamánto looked from her window upon the world outside, when at last she could distinguish sea from mountain, and nearer, could make out the roofs of her friends' dwellings, her eye saw nothing but icicles hanging from tile or spout, signs of the rainy southern gale of yestereen, all frozen, ere dawned at last the morn of Epiphany.

Diamanto, being only a girl, did not think it necessary to get up in time to go to church. Get up she did, however, before sunrise. She lit the fire and put the house tidy, and by the time that the deep blue of heaven grew more open and more clear, she took her stand near the window, with the fire-pan beside her, and there, each wing of the window closed, turned her gaze churchwards.

It was the hour when the congregation goes forth to the river for the casting of the cross. It was impossible to see the people as they emerged from the church, even though (for the distance was not

great) Diamanto could hear the pathetic sound of
their psalmody. But it was not long ere the procession came full in view : first the priests, in their
gold embroidered vestments, gospel in hand, chanting the Baptism of our Lord ; behind them the
acolytes, two and two, bearing each a banner, or the
glittering pictures of the cherubim ; then the singers
and the intoning choir ; and lastly, the never-ending crowd of men and women, the people of three
parishes, all joined for this solemn ceremony, and
so many that the cherubim already sparkled on the
sands ere the last of the crowd were seen. They
looked like a swarm of human ants. When all were
arrived, the solemn rite was to begin. The waters
were to be blest, and then a golden cross cast in, for
which the boldest and hardiest were ready to dive
and fetch it out again.

This scene Diamanto watched with great emotion
and eagerness ; not so much because of the beauty
of the picture—and beautiful it was, with the sun
now slowly rising as the procession halted at the
mouth of the river, a mile or so from the village—
but she knew that somewhere in that crowd was
her lover, the brave young Yannaros, who had passed
all his youth and manhood on the foam of the sea.
He knew not the meaning of fear or cold. Only
the evening before, the eve of the Epiphany, he had

come with some friends to his lover's house to drink
a dram of mastick; and as they drank, she herself
pouring the liquor for them, he had told her that
on the morrow he himself meant to dive in and
bring up the cross.   Diamanto knew him, her
mother knew, and so did Mistress Barbara, all
knew how determined he was.   God forbid that
they should say him nay!   For their hearts went
out to him; and a better husband than he could
none be found.

That is the reason why Diamanto was watching,
with desire and a beating heart.

" How bitter cold!" said she to herself, watching
the steam that rose from the troubled waves out at
sea.

But she looked again at the sun; she looked at
the cherubim flashing in its rays; and marked the
ice on the house-roofs, now beginning to melt and
drip; and consoled herself by thinking, that when
the time came to cast in the cross, it would not be
quite so cold.

Thus passed half an hour or so.   And now her
eyes were fixed more firmly than ever upon the
river.   But so far away, and with a crowd so thick
thronging about the stream, what could she see?
She could see nothing at all, and could distinguish
nothing except the wild throbbing of her own heart.

A little while and the people began to return. Now she arose, and crossed herself, praying our Lady to forgive her that all this time she had neglected the burning of the incense, sitting and gazing as if it were only some common feast day. And as now she waved the censer before the shrine, she gave thanks to our Lady that at last that mad and unreasonable diving was over and done. A sudden thought came that perhaps he was drowned ! Then once more she fell to eager prayers.

"Now for the fire," said she, when this was done. She heaped on the fuel, poking it up, to make all ready for her old mother, who was sure to come in whatever happened, and bring perhaps a neighbour or two, to soak a biscuit in their coffee, and have a chat.

It was broad day by now. The sunshine was everywhere, and everywhere could be heard talking and the sound of voices. And now the girl's heart was at rest, and she sang softly to herself as she went to and fro putting things to rights.

All of a sudden, she drew herself up stiff, her eyes wide open, one hand resting against the wall and the other to her cheek, her ear turned to the door, that she might hear the better. There was no mistake, poor girl ; that sound was the sound of mourning.

Just as she moved towards the door, her unhappy
mother entered, a kerchief wrapped about her face,
and pale as death, panting, like one demented.

"My child, my child! He is gone, our dear
one, our laddie, he is swallowed up in the swollen
river!" She cried aloud, and fell upon the ground,
and not another word.

After her came the women of the neighbourhood,
and came their friends, in came the comrades of
Yannaros; what they could they did, saying what
the heart bids at the time of such calamities; and
the old parish priest came with them, and told
poor Diamanto that it was the Almighty that had
taken her own dear one to his arms; but all in
vain.   From that day lip never smiled within that
house.

KOUTOZAPHIRIS

"HERE is another specimen—Koutozaphíris! And it's not so long since it happened to him. Speak to him, he looks at you with eyes dim as if in a dream. Wait for his answer, and he gives you never a word. The fact is, it runs in the family. His father, too, was always a muddle-head, but only up to a certain point; with this poor fellow there's no limit, and it's all up with him. As for that only son of his, that pretty boy—what a pity! and what a misfortune for his mother!"

"You are mistaken," said I to my friend, who made these remarks to me the other day as the man in question passed slowly by outside, basket in hand. "In this case the madness, if madness it be, has not passed from father to son, but from son to father. The poor fellow came and told me when first he perceived that he was not quite in his right mind. It is a sad story, but you ought to hear it; perhaps it may do you good, as you are yourself fond of flying in a passion.

"It is now five years since Koutozaphiris married.

You remember how bright he was during his first year of wedded life. It was in the second that misfortune came; then it was he told me about it. That little lad was the joy of both of them. His wife, Vasilína, was accustomed every morning to put away the bedding and make the room tidy; then she gave the child in charge of his father, who took him down into the kitchen, sometimes singing him songs, sometimes fondling him. That became quite a part of the round of household duties. Then he would sit by his child's side, feed him, and prattle to him. One morning Koutozaphiris was not quite well, and as ill luck would have it, the child was not well either. The child began to cry. It cried, and the more its father soothed it as he went downstairs, the more the boy screamed. He was cutting his teeth, and it hurt him, he couldn't say what the matter was, so he cried. Zaphiris entered the kitchen, got ready the baby's food, took him up gently. But it was of no use; keep still the child would not. Just as he began to sip his coffee, and perhaps get a little patience, the child began to scream louder than ever. Zaphiris grew wild. He set down his cup, up went his hand, and down it came with a tremendous slap on the child's right ear, which silenced the poor little fellow. In a moment he saw what he had done, but it was too late. He caught him up, kissed him, fondled him, hugged him to his breast. The child was trembling slightly, and blue in the face. Zaphiris was mad with grief, and fear that his wife might find out what he had done. He sprinkled the child with water, dandled him up and down, held him this way and that way, and brought him half back to consciousness, then the poor little one began to cry again. He cried, but not with a full healthy sound as before; this was a kind of low choking murmur. In this pitiful way the child has cried ever since, and so he talks, and laughs, and always will. The box on the ear has made him an idiot.

" His mother did not find out, and I hope she never may, what happened on that ill-omened morning. One called it the evil eye, another I know not what, but the truth she never heard. They brought the unhappy child to me for my opinion. I asked them if it had fallen down and had a blow, if it had been frightened, but no, there was nothing of the sort. I did what I could, but it remained incurable, and will always be so, incurable as the sorrow of the poor mother.

" Well, as to Zaphiris. What torment he suffered when he came to see me some months later, and confessed all to relieve his mind, as he could no longer keep his terrible secret to himself. At

times, he told me, he became as one mad. He
lay awake of nights, and as he thought how he
had had such a little angel in the house, and
for one innocent cry had put out the light of
reason with a savage blow, he, the child's own
father, who loved him as the apple of his eye,
who was so proud of him, who fondled him and
fed him morning by morning like a little bird
—for him (said he) to go and kill the child,
kill three lives at one fell blow—he could stay
in bed no longer. He would rise, telling his
wife that he had lost his sleep again, and go
out into the garden, where he stalked up and
down like a ghost. His wife kept her eye on
him, and saw how he suffered; and thinking
that he was distressed because of the incom-
prehensible illness of the child, forgot the child,
and began to think of the father.

"In the daytime again, Zaphiris, in dire despair,
kept far away from everybody; and there felt the
same torments and misery. He walked he knew
not whither, and sometimes found himself at
another village. Then he would return at the
top of his speed, to get home before evening,
for fear his wife should be alarmed. He would
enter the house to take another look at the
child, which lay subdued, shrinking, pale, with

little to say and ever those low groans, without appetite, without life, with ill-luck in its glances; and he would watch the mother tending it, gazing upon it with grief and yearning, crooning lullabies, turning her tearful eyes towards her husband as he came in, restless, outwearied, despairing! How could a heart bear all that? The heart of Zaphiris broke; he became like the boy, an idiot, shrinking, subdued; his conscience smote him upon the head harder far than that un-forgotten blow which he had dealt to his son; and now no one lives in that deserted home, except the true-hearted wife who cares for him, and bears the burdens of them all!"

UNCLE YANNIS AND HIS DONKEY

If Uncle Yannis has his story, he owes it to that donkey of his. That donkey—Grizzle they called him, and we will call him Grizzle too—that donkey worked well for his living, from the first hour that his back knew the pack-saddle. That donkey Grizzle was a lucky donkey, in spite of all the hard work he did for a livelihood. Grizzle was a donkey of character, and he showed his character when Uncle Yannis had kept him six months harnessed at the winch by his well, six hot summer months that might have taken the heart out of a lion; and for all that Grizzle never lost his strength in that yoke, nor his great voice,—nor the zest with which he enjoyed himself, when from time to time the master loosed him to get a whiff of air in the fields, to refresh himself with the young grass.

When Uncle Yannis lost his garden, nothing was left to him but Grizzle. Grizzle was his friend, his fortune, his mainstay. With Grizzle he worked, to Grizzle he talked. Up and down the hill where

178

the village was he went with his Grizzle, and there was no kind of merchandise, no fodder, fruit, or firewood, that did not go by way of Grizzle's crossed back, before it came into the neighbourhood where Uncle Yannis lived.

It was as though Uncle Yannis and his Grizzle were one and indivisible. Together they ate, together they walked, and they slept together. Right away on the outskirts of the village was Uncle Yannis in a hut all by himself, and Grizzle in the yard. Early in the morning out came Uncle Yannis to the door, and his first good-morning was for Grizzle. Then Grizzle would turn his head towards his master, then pricked up his ears with affection and joy, and looked at him with a roguish twinkle in deep black eyes that any young maiden might have envied.

At other times again, when at work, if the heat was great and the load very heavy, and if Grizzle chanced to be in a bad temper, or annoyed beyond endurance, and so was not so eager as might be for the climb, Uncle Yannis would lose patience with him, and speak to him in words that no man could have endured; and yet Grizzle did endure it, and took no offence; for he knew that Yannis had a stick, though he never used that stick until he saw that words were of no use. The donkey was more

sensible than many men, who never think of giving
way to you, or agreeing with anything, no matter
how reasonable, unless they see and feel your power,
either on their backs or elsewhere.

A heroic donkey was Grizzle, a discreet master
was Uncle Yannis. And that was the reason that
Grizzle lived for many years, and helped his master
as never donkey helped master before.

But everything in this world comes to an end,
and there came an end to the inseparable friendship
of Uncle Yannis and Grizzle.

The loving pair were climbing the hill, one midday, in the month of August, with a load of grapes.
It was the vintage, and they had no time to lose ;
the clusters of fruit lay about in the vineyards, cut
ready to carry off and press, and to be made into
treacle, and must, and wine. This was their third trip.
Three trips more must be made, and no time had
they either to stop half-way or to refresh themselves.
Uncle Yannis was an old man by now, but Grizzle
was older. Grizzle was no longer fresh and skittish
as of yore.

" Quick, you rascal!" cried Uncle Yannis hoarsely
to him. " Quick ! we have three more loads to
carry, and then you shall have melon-rind with
your feed this evening. Hi ! let's get on, you
brute ! "

And Grizzle tried to trot ; but his legs trembled, his ears were down, he gasped. With a gasp he stopped stock still ; his knees gave way, and down he went, his white belly upturned to the sun, his feet in the air, and the baskets of grapes behind him.

Uncle Yannis ran up in distress ; never before had such a thing happened to Grizzle. He began to unloose the fastenings of the load, which was tight round Grizzle's girth, and hindered his breathing. With his knife he cut the fastenings, eased the load as much as he could, then took hold of the halter and tried to pull Grizzle up.

" Come, old boy, get up ; poor fellow, get up, we have three journeys more ! Get up ; you shall have a feed of barley to-night ! You deserve it, poor old chap ! Up with you, my Grizzle ! "

But Grizzle could not get up.

Uncle Yannis stooped, and patted his back, his neck, his snout, and then another pull. But no result ; Grizzle did not get up.

Then a fear came into his mind that something was the matter with Grizzle ; perhaps—and the mere fear made him sit down, to lean against something and take time to recover, to get strong enough to look at his eyes, and see whether he breathed ; to see if his Grizzle were still alive.

He sat panting, overwhelmed with grief, and with the effort of loosening the load, and easing the baskets, with pulling away at the halter to get Grizzle up, with the terrible heat of the sun that blistered him as it beat upon his head.

He sat down ; and get up again he could not. He had only come as far as a rock, half way up the hill, with never a soul in sight to come and pour him a drop of water to help him.

Suddenly he again thought of his poor Grizzle, and tried to crawl to the place where he lay on his side, to coax him and make him get up; to get on his back then and go to his little hut, where they might both rest and let the grapes look after themselves.

But Uncle Yannis could not get up. The more he thought about getting up the deeper he sank in that faintness that had come over him ; deeper and ever deeper ; and now not a thought was left in his mind except the wish to stretch his hand out upon Grizzle, and give him to know that he was near him, that he was tired out too, and that he would lie by his side till they recovered.

The old man gathered all his remaining strength and stretched out his hand.

Heavily fell the hand upon the lifeless neck of Grizzle. As the hand fell, so it lay ; and so lay

the old man, motionless, speechless, insensible.
Not a gleam of light shone now in his exhausted
mind, and not even the ants and the flies could
torment him now.   Only the sun beat upon him
as he slept his everlasting sleep, close by his
Grizzle's side—his heroic Grizzle, who died in har-
ness, like a soldier at his post.

The next day you could see nothing in that
spot but a few grapes scattered about.   The
old man, Uncle Yannis, had been buried at St
Marina's, a little way above, and poor Grizzle had
been thrown over the precipice below.

Grizzle was not buried, even though he had
worked all his life long.   But the birds had pity on
him, and bared all his white bones, and the sun
warmed them, and the rain washed them clean,
until they too disappeared, and nothing at all was
left of poor Grizzle but this little story.

LOVE IN THE TRAIN

A DAY or two since we were in Father Nicodemus'
cell, four monks, and round the fire-pan we talked.
Outside bellowed the storm, and the clearer we
heard it, we huddled all the closer around the fire.
But, apart from the fire, apart from our rum, we
had the summer in our hearts. And even if there
were white hairs in our beards, they only served
the better to set off the ruddy brightness in the
cheek. Our eyes flashed, and on our lips—all that
could be seen of them when we laughed through
the bushy beards—was vivid fun, shrewdness, and
innocent roguery.

We had an hour or two before us ere we need
retire for the night. One of us said, " Lads, we see
little of the world here. We have neither town nor
village, only a hill, with four-and-twenty Brethren
and a few beasts. Of psalms and hymns we have
enough and to spare in church. But a man wants
to see the world sometimes, and I propose, brothers,
that we see the world to-night ; and see it with the
eyes of our mind, since we cannot see it in the flesh.

Come, let one of us tell us the best story of his
experience in the world; bashfulness and lies
avaunt! Let's see how he enjoyed life before he
came under the yoke. There's no wrong in it, so
don't be afraid. He that doesn't do it talks about
it; and he that says nothing thinks the more.
And for us, better than doing or thinking is to talk,
and get it off our minds, and it will serve to pass
the time pleasantly."

This little sermon pleased us all, and we at once
agreed to the proposal. And we agreed that the
proposer himself should tell the story, Father
Timotheos.

So Father Timotheos began as follows:

" My brethren, the story I am about to tell you
is no great affair, but it has remained in my mind,
and nothing could ever remove it. It is now some
fourteen years ago, when I was Deacon to my dear
old Bishop. The poor fellow suffered from a chest
complaint, and at the time travelled to Paris for
the doctors to see it. The doctors saw it, and we
saw Paris with all its glories. After a week's stay,
we took our tickets for Marseilles. As we journeyed
to Marseilles, somewhere about midnight, three or
four hours after the start, the train stopped at a
station; I forgot to tell you that we two had the
carriage to ourselves, the old Bishop and I. The

Bishop was asleep in one corner, and I was sitting
in the other corner and trying to sleep; but the
stoppage of the train awoke me, and I got up to see
where we were. As I looked out, the door opened,
and in got an old gentleman and a damsel with
him. And another man, as old as the first, stood
outside with baskets, bags, bottles, and all that sort
of thing, which he handed in one by one to his
friend, talking all the while in French. What he
was saying I don't know ; but it seemed to me that
the old gentleman outside was the father of the
girl, and the old man who had got in was some
kind of relation, or protector, or guardian. Then
the girl stooped forward and kissed the old gentleman outside, the door closed, and the train was off
again.

"Now, my boys, I must tell you that I was not
a very handsome deacon. But this beard of mine"
—Father Timotheos stroked it as he said the words
—"was black then, and my face was bright with
youth, under my brand-new priest's hat.

"'But the girl,' you will cry, 'we want to hear
about the girl's looks, not yours !'

"Well, now for the girl. Have you ever opened
a casket and suddenly beheld a fine diamond ? Do
you remember how your eyes were dazzled by its
brilliant rays ? Even so did that angel shed radi-

ance around, as she sat in the corner opposite me, in a crimson mantle, and drew up the black veil which covered her lovely face. What eyes she had ! what great blue eyes ! what lips !—like a rosebud trying to open ! Her face was rounded, with a fine contour. And as for colour, you would have called hers the colour of dawn's first blush.

" The girl took her seat, and glanced at us each in turn, the Bishop and me. The old man was still standing before her, and making her comfortable. He must arrange the dark rug over her knees, relieve her of the hat which she took off, showing her golden hair, put a kind of cover about her head, something of blue silk, with patterns in gold embroidered upon it, enough to bewitch you, even if you were a bishop.[1] The Bishop all this while was fast asleep opposite, lying at full length with his head muffled up. And I was the only one who saw it.

" Then the old man took a place beside her, rolled up his own feet in another rug, took off his hat, put on a black travelling-cap, and with a glance at me, and a few words to the girl that might have meant how oddly I was dressed, turned away and closed his eyes. Now and again he half opened them, to see if the girl wanted anything, but she

[1] Bishops are always celibate in the Greek Church.

too was by this time trying to sleep herself. She
was a divine image of beauty, as she lay with her
head inclined to one side, and her eyes closed.

"I pretended to sleep too, and I wanted to sleep.
'What's the use of watching her?' said I to myself.
'She must be a girl just set free from school. Her
eyes are the eyes of a child. She will never set foot
in our Cathedral; and that Cathedral I will never
leave. So good night to her, and sweet sleep. All
the same, I'll open my eyes and see if she is asleep.'

"I opened my eyes; the old man was really
asleep now, and my Bishop the same. But as for
the girl, my eyes seemed to catch a glance of hers.

"Again I closed my eyes. What shall I do now?
open them again? And if she sees me, I shall put
myself to shame. Why shame, however? If she
sees me, she will be looking too. Well, let's open
them and try.

"I opened my eyes once more, and suddenly.
The fair one could not stand it; she shut hers very
quickly, but not before I could see she had been
watching me. Well, what was I to do now I had
made her angry? I must shut mine again, and go
to sleep, and let us all rest.

"Sleep and rest, indeed! The devil himself had
got into me, and poured an unseen fire through my
blood. My head went round, and on trying to re-

peat some prayer to myself, I could not remember a single word. Against my will I fell thinking again of those blue eyes. One more glance, I thought, and then to sleep.

"And once again I opened my eyes : hers were shut ; I might gaze at my ease. My gaze drank in all her maiden beauty. I tried to exert a magnetic influence over her, to awake her, that she might open her eyes and look upon me, now that my mind had no shame left, only longing indescribable.

"And now it was her turn, and all of a sudden she opened her eyes upon me. She saw I was watching her, the witch ! She opened them, and fixed them upon me. This acted as a charm upon me, and I kept mine open too. I beheld her tenderly and calmly, so as to cause no alarm. Her look was full of innocence and of sympathy ; no ill thing could lurk in such a mind as hers. We looked upon each other thus a long time. We gazed, and by degrees the eyes of each began to shine with love and sweetness. We had no reserve left now ; we felt full trust, for each had seen the other's heart. Then even the thought that we were perfect strangers, that after the morrow we should never meet again, this too gave us greater confidence. We gazed, and never felt that we had enough of this blessedness. We fell into a golden dream amid

those long, never-ending looks. Her soul entered
within me, and my soul entered her, and embracing
with our eyes we plunged in depths unfathomable.
Our hearts knew that for us the eye was all, and
other bliss impossible ; and with that skill and
power which the heart alone knows, concentrated
all the joy of love into that union from eye to
eye.

" An hour passed by thus, and the old men still
slept; but her friend did not seem to sleep very
heavily ; if he had, God knows whether I should not
have risen to approach her side.   Indeed, without
thinking, I actually made a movement; like lightning she checked me, with a significant look at her
sleeping friend.   I understood, and made as though
to turn over on the other side, to sleep the easier.
Then we closed our eyes again, both of us ; we
closed our eyes, and when I thought once more to
open them, one loud, long shriek of the engine
awoke us all.

" The old man leaped to his feet ; the Bishop
moved, and began to cough.   The girl got up too
(by this time the train was at a standstill), and
exchanged her embroidered head-cover for the hat ;
the old man collected their traps, and they prepared
to descend.   The man went first ; the girl, as she
followed, threw me a handkerchief."

" Where's the handkerchief now ? " asked Father
Parthenios, impatiently.

" Gone !   I dropt it in the sea on our voyage
from Marseilles.   Why should I keep the handkerchief ?   Brethren, that love was a whole lifetime
to me, though it lasted but an hour.   And the
memory of it has remained deep within my heart,
where no handkerchiefs can be hidden, yet there is
room to hide a whole heaven."

LOVE ON THE HILLS

WHEN Father Timotheos had made an end of his tale, we were all sorry that it was so short, and that there was no second chapter to that story of the train.

"If that's the kind of story you want," said Father Païsios, turning a little, "I could tell you another; only it's rather late, and we ought to go to bed early to-day."

"My dear fellow, what's that?" cried Father Kallínikos; "a winter night, and you're afraid of losing one hour's sleep? Come, tell us your story, and while you talk I'll roast you some chestnuts."

So Païsios began.

"This love in the train, which Father Timotheos has just been describing, puts me in mind of a trip I made from one island to another, selling crucifixes from Mount Athos. I was travelling on one occasion from Imbros to Lemnos, in order to get a passage across here; not much of a journey that. A little journey, but a big storm! I had as fellow-travellers a certain family, father, mother, two boys and one girl, They were going to be present at a wedding.

" Hardly had we left the harbour when the dance began. The caique was tossed up and down like a bit of melon-peel on those maddened waves, the tackle creaked, the sails flapped in the wind, and the water dashed up on us and poured over the gunwale like a river. Not a soul was on deck, except the sailors ; everybody else was down below, and imagine how happy we were! As if the trouble outside was not enough, there were the women shrieking. And the vows they made to the Holy Mountain ! I am always quite comfortable at sea, so I thought I would go on deck, to huddle down in some quiet corner, come what would ; but I was rather afraid that the sailors might lay the storm on my shoulders, and say I had brought it[1] ! So I stayed below after all, and spent the time in watching these poor folk from Imbros. Sometimes I brought them water, sometimes I arranged their pillows, and so the hours passed. At last night came on, and we went to sleep.

"Towards dawn the caique suddenly became quiet. We heard shouts up on deck, ' hurry up ' and ' look alive there,' talking, the captain's orders, and last

---

[1] It is a common superstition of sailors that a priest on board brings ill-luck.

of all the anchor. We could not have arrived so soon, with such a tempest, and the wind from the north ; we must have cast anchor somewhere until the storm should pass. I hurried up on deck, and what should I see but the coast of the mainland somewhere over against Tenedos! We had gone back instead of forwards.

"We all went up on deck. All around was a wilderness, wild mountains covered with trees, in which were birds whose song reached us by the strand, and what a strand! There was not a print of human foot on that virgin shore, nothing but long lines one above the other, made by the waves on the white sand.

"We got out our provisions, the women lighted a fire behind a rock a little further inland, and then we sat and breakfasted. Then our skipper told us we should stay there till midday, when the wind would change. Well, we did what we could to fill up the time ; one went this way, one the other, until midday should come.

"The skipper and the old Imbriote went off to the right with a gun, as there was said to be good sport there. The boys with their sister, who was about sixteen, went straight inland, where there were said to be flowers. The mother, a woman who could not yet have past her fortieth year,—so much said

her bright eye and ruddy lip, apart from other signs
which there is no need to mention in such a company as this,— she stayed behind to collect her
belongings and give them to the cabin-boy to put
on board. I thought I would follow the others
towards the right, and stroll after the hunters.
But down to the left something caught my eye on
the top of a little hill, something that might be a
chapel, or a shepherd's hut, or anything of that
sort. Well, I thought I would go and find out
what it was; and thither I wended my way. In
half an hour I was at the spot. It was neither
shepherd's hut nor deserted chapel; a heap of
stones piled one upon another, a rock with a wild
olive tree on the other side, and in the middle a
trench with musk and other such plants growing in
it. There I took my seat and looked around me,
mightily refreshed by those virgin beauties, inimit-
able, innumerable. About this time the wind had
fallen, and the sea below was a picture of happiness.
And there, as I sat, what should I see before me
but the Imbriote woman!

"'God bless you, my good woman, what do you
want here?' said I. 'Don't you see that here we
are together alone, and your husband may come
and throw us both into the sea? Back with you
if you love your children; back, ma'am, and pluck

flowers with them; and I'll stay here till midday,
for such beauty as this one does not see every day
in the year!'

"'Tut, tut, why shouldn't I stay, too, Father!
Haven't I got a pair of eyes as well as you? As
for my husband, you needn't be afraid. I lost my
way, and I didn't know where I was coming. Your
holiness will go down this way, and I'll go that;
one of us will start half an hour before the other;
and there you are. Not a soul can see us here."

"And down she sat close beside me and gave
me a mischievous look.

"And God above?" said I.

"God never told us not to have a little love
now and again."

"And she leant against me as she spoke, panting
from the climb, with cheeks red as a rose, it might
have been from the exercise, it might have been
for some other reason—and eyes brighter than
ever.

"I recognised that here was a terrible temptation;
for I was still young; and although I had weathered
some of these delightful tempests in my young
days, now that I wore this black hat, brethren, I
had no intention of disgracing it for the sake of a
woman's momentary whim. So up I got from the
rock on which I was sitting, turned to look in the

opposite direction, when all of a sudden a notion
came into my head which I felt I must put in
practice immediately, if I was to save myself. To
turn and look at her, or address her again, was
destruction ; well, to avoid seeing her, I must just
go straight down the hill that way. "I must go
aboard the boat, take my bag, and make the best
of my way to Niochóri, which was about three
hours' walk away, as one of the sailors had told
me. Thus I would get off once for all from the
enchantress.

"No sooner thought than done. The fair one
hadn't time even to call me back ; I had got well
rid of her, and took the downward road.

"The children were still gathering flowers, the
sailors were mending the rents in their sails, the
hunters were firing away inland, and I, bag on
shoulder, tramped alongshore to Niochóri ; and I
recollect how I sang the hymn 'From my youth, O
Lord,' as a kind of triumphal chant, as though
telling our Saviour that he had saved me again,
glory be to Him.

"From Niochóri I found means of crossing to
Tenedos, and there I was rewarded for my virtue
with the generous wine which they gave me there
to drink."

AUNT YANNOULA

It is now many years since the old serving woman
whom you see came into this house from a village
on the opposite shore. She must have seen much
and suffered much in her day. Look at her great
bright eyes, like two withered pansies, brows thick
and black as a leech, a firm and decided mouth,
pale face which not even the bright reflection of
the fire can redden. She looks a real witch with
that kerchief over her head and the yellow apron.
She cuts up the meat with a look of bitterness on
her face; you could easily imagine her to be
concocting a poison.

Very different is the young girl slicing quinces
beside her. She is the darling of her father,
because she is supposed to be like him. She has
his gray eyes and rounded chin; but her father
has not the same beauty, I imagine. When he
tucks up his sleeves, and his darling daughter pours
water for him to wash, you do not see a fine pair
of white arms twinkling over the silver bowl. The
girl has her mother's beauty, they say. Such pure

beauty is the only true ornament of a girl's face.
She is very fond of the old servant Aunt Yannoula.
When the others are playing or singing, off she
runs to the kitchen and helps Yannoula. And
Yannoula lets the girl do it, in order that the
master may hear of it afterwards, and be glad that
his dear daughter has made the quince marmalade
again.

Now they have put on the pot, and the dinner
is boiling. The old dame sits down on her cushion,
and takes up her distaff; the girl is beside her.
The old woman has something to say ; let us hear
what it is.

"This is not the first time, nor the second,
that you have plagued me to tell my story. You
are only a little girl, and why should I pain you ?
But you will insist upon hearing it. Well, you
shall hear it, only be sure you never breathe a
word to any one, or my curse will consume you.
No one knows of it but your parents.

"The village I come from lies many a long league
away. Ah, my poor home! I have never seen it
since I left. Our cottage was not in the village
itself ; it stood outside, in a thick grove of trees.
The pasture was up on the hill, and there my
uncle Nicóles tended his flock of goats. He it was

gave me a dower and found a husband for me. I had been an orphan for years, when he took to me, and gave me my dear Giorgis. My wedding portion was the hut where we lived, one plot of land, and half the old man's goods. The old man lived along with us. God did not see fit to bless us with children, but we had all other blessings. Ah, the Almighty knew what he was doing; may He continue to bless us !

"One evening, the old man had gone up to his fold—it was springtime then, just as it is now—to see if Giorgis had got the flock under shelter, as a violent shower of rain was coming on. As for me, that was not the first time I had been left alone in the house; I got dinner ready, and sat spinning just as I am doing now. The old man had hardly left when all was uproar; thunder and lightning, flash on flash; I made the sign of the cross, and huddled over the fire. Quicker than I can tell you, the rain came in torrents; and no sooner had it begun to fall, than who should come tumbling into the cottage but a couple of Turks ! One look at them, and a kind of madness came over me; their cruel laugh at seeing me alone in the place was more terrible even than their faces or the weapons they wore. At first I thought they had just come in for shelter until the rain ceased ; but that was not what they wanted. Whether they struck out the idea on the instant, or whether they had planned it out all before, God alone knows. The first thing they did was to shut the door; when I noticed this, I would have risen, but I felt a faintness which made me fall back, distaff in hand; I could not utter a word. But I was strong and healthy, and the faintness soon passed. When I began to recover consciousness, I observed that they were trying to pull me up and get away. They were afraid, as it seemed, that some one might surprise them and prevent their design, and so they thought it best to carry me off to some more solitary place. The rain had now nearly ceased. The first thing I can dimly remember is how one of them lifted me, while the other opened the door. When they had done this, and dragged me over the threshold, I heard a pistol-shot. Ah, and the heart-rending cry I heard next, 'Yannoula! Yannoula!' Never shall I forget that bitter cry of woe as my husband called me. He must have run down, poor fellow, and got to the cottage without meeting the old man.—He never spoke again.

Now that I was more awake, I began to realise the awful thing that had happened to me, like a bolt from the blue. You must not suppose, though, that I uttered a cry or crooned a lament. For my heart had grown hard and fierce, and made the woman into the man. I became suddenly strong, and turned away. Such a fire blazed up within me, that I felt as if I could shake them off, and seize and throttle them. Shake them off I did, and threw myself down upon my poor dear, my darling husband. It seemed to me that he still trembled a little. For a moment I forgot those brutes beside me; my heart softened, I stooped down and touched his face, that I might kiss him, and speak to him, ask where the wound was — a thousand things I wanted to do in that one instant, and I had not time to do one! One of the men seized me by the waist, the other grasped my arm, and with curses and threats they dragged me through the outer gate. I thought of crying out, on the chance that some one might hear and save me; but I was afraid the old man should be near, and if he appeared they might kill him too. There were no other neighbours in that lonely place. Then again I feared they might gag me. So I saw that my only chance lay in a trick.

"'Where are you taking me now," I asked them, " in all this hurricane? Wait a bit till the weather

clears, and then you may do what you like. My
husband lies there with a bullet in him; who is
there to be afraid of?'

"Well, child, they carried me in again, and like
a pair of wolves they fell on the food I had cooked.
I left them to their meal alone, and with a light in
my hand went to the door for another look at my
George. He was quite still now, and his chest all
over blood : my darling was dead. As I stood
looking at him, senseless as a stone, out came those
dogs again and dragged me in ; they were afraid I
might give them the slip.

"Two thoughts were tormenting me just then ;
the first, how I could save the old man ; the other,
how to kill the murderers of my husband.

"The Turks were strangers, and did not know
us. They must have been travelling by way of our
village, and lost their way ; and when they were
caught in the storm they ran for refuge to our
cottage. There were no such devils as those
in our neighbourhood. As for our Turks, the
worst they did was to lift a goat now and
again.

"I closed the door, and tried to look as though
they had nothing to fear now. They began to grow
confident, and set about enjoying themselves in good
earnest. I got out wine for them (our jar was never

empty); but before I gave it to them, I added some
spirit. The wine must act quickly, before the old
man should return, and there was no other way.
My heart went pit-a-pat, for fear his knock should
come before they were drunk. It was soon done;
one dropt forward, the other let his head fall back,
and stared at the ceiling, mumbling incoherently.
Taking the chopper, I hit one over the nape of the
neck, the other full on the throat. I never trembled.
I did the job as coolly as if I had been a butcher.
My heart was a stone. I stood looking at them,
and feeling as happy as a queen, forgetting that I
was a miserable widow. Just at that moment,
there came Uncle Nicoles to the door with a
dripping sack over his shoulders. He stood stock
still, petrified, as though he was in a dream.
When I turned about and saw him, I was a
woman again in a moment, and burst out
weeping. The poor fellow nearly went mad
when I told my story.

"'What are you doing there?' says he. 'We
must get away, or we are lost!'

"'Where can we go to?' I asked. 'How can
we leave my poor Giorgis?'

"We went out and carried him indoors. Ah,
how can I ever forget his bitter smile? It
must have remained upon his face ever since I

fell beside him, and felt to see whether he still lived !

"I cannot describe to you that awful night, child ! We decided to stay, and not to run away. We went out to the furthest corner of our little field, where a tall sycamine grew ; it was dark as pitch, by good luck there was no moon. For hours the old man dug, while I shovelled away the earth. And our terror ! if a leaf fell, we trembled. When the pit was as deep as my waist, we returned to the cottage and carried out the bodies just as they were, with their arms and all. Another half hour, and those two butchered beasts were buried, and the new-dug earth covered over with twigs and brushwood.

"And now only my dead husband's body was left in the house. We washed his breast, and threw the bloody clothes into the fire ; we laid him out, and arrayed him in his shroud for burial.

"The dawn was breaking as we began to wash away the blood-stains, the old man cleaning the stones outside, and I the floor of the cottage. And as the sun looked over the storm-beat hills, and the world began again to smile, we sat down for the first time after all those terrible hours, wide

awake though utterly weary, trembling, broken-
hearted.

"There is no need to say much more ; besides,
master may come in any moment. No one had the
least suspicion of the truth. My husband had been
struck by lightning, and killed ; that was our story.
In the afternoon we buried him. When I returned
home I found that I could not remain in the cottage
by night. I saw their ghosts all around me. I
wanted to get away out of their sight. The old
man was afraid of me ; he threw a pair of
saddle-bags over his shoulders, and we departed
together ; he brought me straight over here, as
he knew the master. He went back himself, as
he feared no ghosts, and in that same cottage
he lived until the year before last, when he
passed away. I have never been there since,
nor shall I ever go again. I shall die here
with you.—Don't cry, child, don't tremble. I
have done wrong, and I am a wicked woman
to frighten you."

.   .   .   .   .

It had grown late as this awful tale was told.
The poor girl was terrified and in tears ; her heart
scarcely beat. Why torment the poor thing with
such stories ? Must the innocent and the young
learn of the hell in which their grandmothers lived ?

Of all that hear, who profits thereby? At most
they are glad that such things do not happen in
their day, and that now the Turks, do what they
may elsewhere, no longer spread such havoc amid
our conquered homes.

PANAYIS KALOYANNIS

PANAYÍS KALOYÁNNIS was a good worker in the
War of Independence. I have sought his name
in history, but in vain; I have never seen it in
any book.

Panayis was nephew to a certain Abbot, and to
this Abbot he owes his chief peculiarity, which, as
we shall see later, became his chiefest claim to
remembrance. This peculiarity was that, in season
and out of season, his mind held one sole idea, and
he never said anything but this : " One day our Constantine will sprout up again." At last every one
used to look at him, and sing in their turn : " Constantine shall sprout up again."

He was an orphan, and must have been about
twelve years old when the Abbot took him to his
monastery to educate him. Father Paisios was a
monk, true, but he knew something of life. He
had been to Russia in his young days ; after that
he had been travelling, and ' fishing for friends." [1]
Now he and his gout were resting in the cloister,

---

[1] *i.e.*, enrolling members of the Friendly Society.

and he kept his hands busy with letters and pamphlets ; and in the evening he used to settle himself comfortably on his couch, and tell Panayis the tales of our national history. He did not even forget Pelopidas and Timoleon. The lad heard all this with delight. From ancient times the old Abbot came down by degrees to Byzantium, and one evening he told him of the fall of Constantinople. And when he had told him all, he went on :

" Do you remember, my boy, those grand deeds I told you about last year ? Many and many an evening has passed since then, and never again have we been able to find a Codrus or a Leonidas. Now and again the nation has produced some wild spirit ; but where are the terrible lions of the old days ? You might well have imagined that the brave old Grecian blood was exhausted and dead. Yet all of a sudden, in the year 1453, on May 29th, one Tuesday morning, down drops a hero among us, and holding a rusty sword in his hand, see him scatter the Janissaries as he dashes through one of the gates into the city, like a ravening monster ! See him fall upon them alone, obscure as Codrus, but desperate as Leonidas ! What does that tell you, my boy ? Why, that our race has as many lives as a cat, and if there's only one drop of the blood left, it will grow to a deluge, and overflow the land. And if it had been written in our fate that this divine blessing should have been granted us a few years before Urbanus placed his cannon outside the city, he would never have been able to crush it; but he would have been crushed to pieces himself along with Mahomet's head. But it came too late for us; too late came the inspiration, my son, and it fell into that infinite sea of blood, and was lost!"

As he said the words, Paisios sobbed. The lad looked him in the eyes, and remained silent. When he had looked at him earnestly a little while, he suddenly said:

"Never mind, uncle, one day our Constantine will sprout up again!"

That is the end of the first chapter of the story; and now, with your good leave, we will proceed to the second.

Six years later we find Panayis a well-grown young fellow, sailing about from island to island in a little schooner. Old Paisios, a year before his death, had made him partner with a certain Kapetan Vaglis, and they used to take in a cargo at one island to sell it at the next. But the mind of Panayis was always away at Constantinople. His great delight was to sit down with the men, and tell them about Constantine's end. And after it

was all done, he would tell them his prophecy, that
one day Constantine would sprout up again.

On one of these trips, it so happened that a man
from Psara was on board—Karathanásis, they called
him.   He was not a sailor, but a passenger from
Samos to Psara.   It was just at the time when the
smoke of that seven years' fire was beginning to
rise.

When this man heard Panayis' story, instead of
laughing with the rest, he took Panayis aside, and
said :

" I say, will you join with me in a little job ?
Split partnership with Kapetan Vaglis, and come
along with me.   I follow the same business, but
just now my schooner is hired out to the *ploughmen*."

" Ploughmen ? "   Panayis was puzzled.

" Those who are going to sow the seed of your
Constantine, silly cuckoo!   Do you suppose a
prince will   ever   sprout   up   unless you   sow
blood ? "

Heaven opened, and revealed the truth to Panayis
Kaloyannis.   For years he had prophesied the sprout-
ing of a Constantine, and his mind had never gone
a step further.

" I will ! " was his answer.

When they arrived in Psara, Panayis separated

from his skipper, and joined hands with Karathanasis.

There were two things in the world that this man loved: his country and his daughter. His plan was to betroth Panayis to both, and he did it.

At the beginning it seemed as though of the two loves which Panayis had, the dearer was Marió, the beautiful maid of Psara; and he was eager for marriage.

"Not yet," said her father. "First let us take the schooner, and work her by ourselves, and then we shall come back with a blessing to a *free* Psara. Our freedom will not wait long. Have you forgotten what we did the other day in Eressos?"

So Mario stayed behind with her mother, and the two skippers sailed off together in their ship.

This is the end of the second chapter; and now we shall begin the third.

Twelve months the schooner plied upon the sea, and they sailed to and fro, now with powder, again with biscuit. When the ships sailed, they went round with their vessel; and after she had come to anchor, and her cargo was out, Panayis would find some excuse for going aboard a warship, and there he would gather the men about him to tell them his stories. " Here he is with us now, our Constantine ! " said he once, near Psara, when Kanáris was returning from Chios. " This Constantine will will bring the other to life ! " And the sailors lifted him on their shoulders in their joy.

That trip they ran in and anchored at Psara after a twelvemonth's cruise. Panayis had some hope that Karathanasis would let him marry now ; and one day he told his desire.

" You will say we have our Constantine safe now," said the old man ; " well—but let us make one more journey, and then we'll see."

Panayis, talking to the mother about this, said to her, " I knew what he meant ; he wants me to smell powder first. So I kiss thy hand, and good-bye ! " He longed for a few words with his lover ; but how durst he ? In those days love had neither words nor kisses ; at most there was a glance of the eyes in secret.

It was evening when this conversation took place, and in the morning Karathanasis saw Panayis ready to set out.

" Whither away ? " asked he.

" This time," answered Panayis, " you must take the schooner out by yourself ; I am going with Kanaris."

" Silly boy, talk sense ! " replied the old man.
" Do you want to go and fall in the fire ? "

" Why not, father ? You won't allow me to
marry Mario yet, so let me marry the fire."

So he strutted along with Kanaris' brave boys,
dressed Turkish fashion like the rest of them ; and
off they went to Tenedos.

When he came back from that trip he was wild
with joy. He was never tired of telling that
famous stratagem—how the Kapetan Pasha[1] received
them with open arms ; how he recognised them
when one of my brigs took fire, and slipped his
cables to get away to Stamboul. And happen what
would, he always came back to Constantine.

Like the beast that has had a taste of human
blood, that takes to the hills and the woods to find
another such meal, so Panayis could not keep away
from the sea. No one knew where he was to be
found ; he turned up everywhere, he fought everywhere. For fourteen months he was lost, and never
came near his bride's father or his house.

One evening—it was New Year's Eve, the last
day of '23—there he was, like a corpse risen from
the tomb. His head was bandaged, and one arm
in a sling hung about his neck ; his face yellow.
He had been brought over by a ferry from Moschon-

[1] The Turkish Admiral.

nisi. They had found him lying somewhere on the coast of the mainland, almost dead; indeed he had been left there for dead by his comrades, though luckily for him there had not been time to bury him.

" Now I have become such a hideous object," said he, with a bitter smile, " you won't want me to marry into your family." His knees almost gave way beneath him as he spoke. " Come, lay something for me to fall on, and let me wish you a happy new year. I doubt whether I shall see the morrow." Three days in the boat, and the blood dripping all the while. The whole way from Moschonnisi here is marked by the drops. Ah! how I wish Constantine might be able to see that red line when he comes one day travelling over his seas!"

Then Panayis Kaloyannis lay down and became unconscious; by-and-bye he began to rave in delirium. All night long his friends were on the move. Now and again he came to himself, with a glance at Mario, and then a glance at her father, as if asking whether he ought to look at the girl in such a state.

With the morning Panayis began to recover a little. Then Karathanasis sent at once for the priest, who came, and after seeing the sick man, prepared the Communion.

"Marriage service first, if you please," says the old man; " you can give him the Communion after. We have no time to lose.

The priest stared at him in amazement.

" Marry them, father," says he again, "and be quick about it."

So the priest donned his stole, and crowned the pair.

From that moment Panayis began to get better.

One more chapter, and my story is done.

Six months passed before Panayis was able to get about. It was a summer morning, the twenty-first of the harvest, when he found himself able for the first time to cross the threshold with Mario, and to sit down and watch the sun rise. The old man had been absent overnight at Paliókastro in company with many others. His dame was doing the household work, and the newly married pair were chatting with the neighbours. Suddenly they heard the sound of a cannonade from the sea : it was the guns of Hosref Pasha which greeted Psara on that unforgotten morning.

They all leapt to their feet, all but poor Panayis ; running here, there, and everywhere to see what was afoot. Before long they could discern Turkish standards on the hills over by Ftelio. Then the eyes of the poor Psariots were opened.

Like a flock of goats down they ran helter-skelter
to the sea for safety ; and in the midst of that terrified drove you might have seen poor Mario with
her husband on her shoulders, and her old mother
behind. In vain their eyes searched high and low
for the old father ; he could not get near them.

The Janissaries had taken them completely by
surprise ; no one could understand how they came ;
they seemed to have sprung up out of the ground.
In a very short time they were upon them.

" Down to the sea ! " cried Panayis : " straight to
the sea ! Perhaps we may find a boat."

To the beach they came ; wherever a boat could
be found there was a mass of people, treading each
other down, struggling to get it. Their cries rang
to the heavens.

" Look here," says Panayis to Mario, " this kind
of thing won't do. Drop me down, and run off
with your mother ; don't be afraid about me, I have
been in their clutches before. Put me down, d'ye
hear ? Either you drop me, or I will strangle you ! "

" Strangle me if you like, so long as you are
saved," said Mario, under her breath.

" Run into the sea, then ! There's no boat; see,
they are all gone. Straight into the sea, or they
have us ! They will make you a slave, poor dear,
and then woe to you ! Into the sea with you !

That's right, into deep water. Stop one moment
—your brooch with that coin of Constantine,
where's your brooch ? Put it in my hands. Kiss
it first, then let me kiss it. Mother ! where's your
mother ? Ah, they have her, poor thing ! That
comes of looking behind to find her man, and the
dogs have caught her ! They will not spare her
life, not they. Never mind, mother dear, we are
coming too, don't worry. Now for the plunge,
Mario mine, my love ! Thou too, my golden
Constantine, hide thyself in the sea. Thy day is
not yet come, but it will come, it will . . ."

His voice was drowned in the waves.

The old father was not long in following, but by
another and more cruel way. He passed with
thousands of others through smoke and flames, and
winged his way on high, to find there the liberty
which earth denied him.

IBRAHIM

The most part of those who changed faith in the
dark days of Greece, did so for fear of roasting on
the spit. I do not speak of the poor little ones,
who were innocent enough. The parents, of
course were not innocent; and their mistake lay
in preferring the sword's point to the hilt. For
centuries Greece was all but dead. It was not all
fate; there was a lack of manliness in the nation,
and we paid for it. But that story may be left for
another time; now let us come to Ibrahim.

Ibrahim was a Greek who embraced Islamism
without compulsion. He did it of his own free
will. Perhaps you may think he was a child. No.
he was not a child, but he was in love, which is
the same thing.

His real name was Elias. He was the beloved
son of a village chief; the most handsome lording in
the village was he, and a scapegrace to boot. Who
is the one is generally the other, be it lad or lass.
So Ibrahim dealt havoc throughout the whole village.
But perhaps the village liked it. If a girl does not

want to be teased she is left alone ; and so with a village.

His father was rich, and even the Turks had a wholesome awe of him. He was one of those chieftains who could speak Turkish, ate their food Turkish fashion, and took their pleasure like Turks ; but there were in him many points of the true Greek, things which are not seen like the turban or the fez.

Men like this were wise in their generation. Times came when they gave help to the country, saved some one from the pit, or defended our priceless privileges. And thus, protecting these and saving those, in their old age they became true Greeks in all points.

The chief once had occasion to visit a certain Hassan Aga, and he took his son with him. This was not the first time that the Aga had seen Elias, but it would seem he had not taken much notice of him before ; for this time he killed a lamb for them, and did the honours as an Aga should do. Afterwards he persuaded Elias to sing. A sweet voice had Elias, and a good heart; and as he sang to them the Aga was enchanted. "No one," said he, turning to the lad's father, "no one but a Greek lad could sing so sweetly and so cleverly." On their departure, he escorted his guests to the gate.

As they went out, the boy turned once more to
do obeisance to his Excellency: and, as ill luck
would have it, his eye fell on the lattice of the
harem in one corner of the court.   This lattice did
not quite fill the window ; on one side was an opening
of some size, and from this opening peeped a face,
bright as a sunbeam, and disappeared like a flash
of lightning.   It was the beauteous Melek, only
daughter of Hassan Aga.

From that hour Elias knew no peace.   Not a
moment could he rest quiet indoors.   He listlessly
roamed about the fields, as near as he durst to the
Aga's grand house.   What he wanted he did not
know himself.   To break through the walls and get
into the harem without being seen of eunuch or
slave, and to fall at Melek's feet and cry "I love
thee !" would be about as easy as to take Stamboul
by storm.

Now the Aga too had his own pangs ; he too had
a trouble to eat his heart.   O that he might become
an eagle, and fly away to Olympus with the lad !
From the chibouk to the Koran, from the Koran
to a governorship—step by step the Greek lad
might become an Aga.   For his Excellency this
would be no difficult task.   But the old chief had
teeth, and the plan required tact.   At last the Aga
hit on the device of sending for the lad to teach

him Greek. He wished to learn Greek because he liked the Greek people; he wished them well, and he ought to understand their grievances.

When the old chief came home and heard all this, he seemed ten years older. He told it to his wife, and she with tears told her Elias. Elias listened, and knit his brows; then without a word he set out for the Aga's house.

The Aga was out at Council at the moment; so Elias waited him in the courtyard. And as he waited in the courtyard, he softly sang, with a glance now and then at the enchanted casement. It was not long before the sun rose once more, and shed its beams through that aperture in the lattice. Elias looked round him; there was no one but a single eunuch, and he stretched on the stone seat, and snoring, with his face turned towards the door. Not another soul was to be seen, nor a sign of life at any of the windows, save only in that one corner, where he caught glimpses of a lock of hair, or a white hand, and now and again the corner of an eye which made the blood run madly in the veins of Elias.

There was no time to lose; he must make it clear that he had lost his heart to her, and that for her he was ready to lay down his life. Speak to her? — God forbid! Write? — the prophet had

made that hope vain, in forbidding a Turkish maid
to touch pen or paper. There was nothing left for
it but song ; and he sang to her in Turkish, softly,
softly, and clear, that she might understand. These
were the last words of the song :

"What time the Pleiades set over the hill, let the houri of
the morning come to the clump of willows, to sprinkle with
dew the wings of the nightingale which longs for her."

There were no willows near but a few that grew
by the brook, not many paces from the Aga's door.

The song ceased, and Elias waited to hear
whether the answer would be life or death. It
was life.

"*Beki eï, Kouzoum, beki eï*," murmured a sweet
voice behind the lattice. "Take care, take care,
the Aga is coming !"

Elias turned, and saw the Aga walking along the
shore. He went forth to meet him. The Aga was
much pleased when he saw him.

"And where are your books ?" he asked.

"Books, Effendim," said Elias; "from our books
you will learn nothing at all. I learnt Turkish by
talking with our neighbour Latif; and Latif learnt
Greek by singing songs with me. But to sing with
your honour would hardly be fitting. So we can
talk together of an afternoon as you return from
the Council. In that way you will learn our language beautifully."

" Good," said the Aga, stroking his beard, " very good, so we will. And you will come in afterwards with me, and have a drink of sherbet."

" Effendim, if I do they will be all saying that I have turned Turk. For my part, I do not care if I do change my religion if it will please you; but I am thinking of my poor old mother, who would go down with sorrow to the grave,"

" No, my son," said the Aga, " I will never bid you become one of us against your will. But one thing I will tell you, and hide it deep in your heart : if ever you do decide upon it, you need fear no one, so long as I am alive."

Elias looked at him with a serious air, greatly moved, and made him a low salaam.

The cunning Aga quite understood with whom he had to deal. " His father's son," he thought to himself; " patience and time will be necessary here."

" Very good, *ogloum*," said he ; "——my son ; we begin to-morrow."

And the Aga went indoors, while Elias took the path by the seashore, singing as he went :

> " *Ghiderim, ghiderim, yoloom deskenmez,*
> *Ardima bakarim serdaim ghurenmez !* "
> " Onward and onward for ever I fare :
> Mine eye looks behind me, my love is not there ! "

His love was not to be seen, true ; but for all
that, his love saw him. Melek saw that he did not
go towards the village, where his mother was waiting for him, but to the brook and the willows.
There he turned and sighed ; walked up and down,
to and fro, sat down and uprose again, until the
sun sank to rest and the stars were sprinkled about
the sky. He watched the setting of the Pleiades, and
counted each moment of the never-ending hours. It
seemed to him like a dream ; was he not mad, he
asked himself, to wait all these hours for an Aga's
daughter to come and meet him among the willows ? Melek, who had never been seen by sun or
moon ?

And then as these thoughts were passing through
his mind, he heard a quiet footfall among the dead
leaves. Elias trembled. He began to quiver with
longing because of his hidden joy. Then she had
understood his song, and her " *Beki eï* " was not an
idle word ! The steps came nearer and nearer, until
he saw before him the form of a woman covered
with a cloak. He essayed to speak, but his tongue
clove to the roof of his mouth. He ran to catch her
in his arms, that he might sit by her side and
smother her with his kisses ; but the girl stretched
out her hand with a gesture of fear, and bade him
keep his distance : she had a message to give, and

for that she had come. She was the faithful and well-beloved slave of the all-beautiful Melek, sent to say that the girl's heart craved no night-shadowed passion, but the love of a whole life ; her life, she said, was in his hands ; but there was only one way to win her—he must become a follower of the Prophet, and then she would be his own.

The maid departed, and Elias was left dumb and desolate. How long he remained there, I know not ; but I know that when he came home, his father and the men were returning with torches quenched after a night's search for the missing son. He found some explanation, half truth, half falsehood, and no more of it at that time.

But his mother was not satisfied. She questioned her son again and again, where he had been all night.

" I went to a tryst, if you must have it, with the fairest fair of all the village, fairest and wealthiest ! All night I waited, and she came not. Now I am going to seek her father, to ask for his daughter's hand. Your son needs no matchmakers ! He will carry the matter through by himself. As for your fears of yesterday, be at rest —I am not a child."

His mother, had she heard a word of such loves at another time, would have rent her clothes that he would not allow her to find him a bride of her own choosing : but now said nothing : only crossed herself, thankful that her fear had been wide of the mark, and that her son had not fallen into the hands of the Turks. And before she had time to ask who was this enchantress, Elias disappeared.

Straight to the great house he went. The Aga had just ended his ablutions, and was drinking his cup of coffee. At first he looked on the lad with no friendly eye, for the opium fumes were still about his wits ; however, he bade him be seated and ordered coffee for him.

" Effendi mine !" said the bright youth, "it will seem strange to you that I pay visits so early ; but this will show that my business is of importance. My life is in your hands !"

" What is it *janoum*—my soul ?" asked the Aga.

" You remember what you promised me yester-day—when I was resolved, I was to inform you ?"

The Aga knit his brows in a frown.

" And your mother ?" said he. " Who wants to have her misery on his conscience ? And your father, too ?"

" Pardon me, Effendi mine ! My father is him-self half a Moslem ; my mother will weep and wait, and in the end she will grow calm. Suppose I were dead—What could she do then? Here there is a choice betwixt two—the Prophet, or death !"

The Aga stood still, and looked him full in the eyes.

"And who will kill you if you do not change your faith ?"

"Love ! Yesterday I entered your courtyard. Up at the lattice of the window in the corner was a white kitten that played with the sprays of jasmine. Suddenly the kitten slipped, and fell into the court. A face peeped out, a glance, a voice—it was gone !"

At this the Aga turned and strode in fury towards the harem.

"Mercy ! Effendi mine ! stop ! If some one must be punished, you must punish me, because I had eyes and saw her ; and not a creature whom the sun has never seen ! Plunge your dagger in my bowels, that you may never need say that a man has seen your daughter, and lives !"

The Aga stood still, and looked angrily upon him.

"Have you no dagger with you ? Here is mine ; plunge it into my heart !—Yet, remember your promise of yesterday : remember what I shall be if I become your son ! Remember that you have no

son of your own! Think what a terror is the
Greek who becomes a Moslem; think in what
hands you will leave your power when Allah shall
one day call you to himself!"

Now the Aga softened, and ere long he was
sitting again on his couch. Elias said no more.
He bowed his head, and awaited the Aga's
word.

"My son," said the Aga at last, "be well
advised in this matter. Think of your mother, and
your mother's curse. What blessing can you
expect after such a curse as that? It will consume you to ashes, both you and us!"

"A thousand curses will fall harmless before the
power of your Prophet! The Prophet wishes that
I should be his! It was the Prophet made that
kitten fall!"

To this, of course, the Aga had nothing to
answer. He rose and embraced the young man,
and sent for the tambourines.

An hour or two later, tambours and pistol-shots
woke the echoes in the village. It was the signal
of the circumcision of Ibrahim.

What happened in the house of Elias' parents
when the news came, not that their son was
about to apostatise, but that he had done so
already, and that he was to wed the daughter of

Hassan Aga? That is another tale in itself, a long and a miserable tale.

Ten days lasted the wedding festivities of Ibrahim and Melek. Ten days the physicians came and went at the house of the ill-starred chief. Ibrahim, intoxicated with the love of his far-famed beauty, neither asked nor bid any one tell him news of his home. On the day when the tambours ceased to sound in the Aga's house, that very day a funeral procession came forth from the house of the chief. The unhappy father could not bear up under this thunderbolt which fell on his grey head. His wife lived after him a few months, to give time, as it would seem, for her to curse her son root and branch.

Say what you will, you must believe sometimes in the power of the curse. If there be nothing in it, tell me how it came about that in three months Melek lay dead? Why did the Aga go mad, so that they bound him hand and foot, and scourged him mercilessly for a cure, but never a cure was for him? Why did Ibrahim himself come nigh to losing his senses, and sold his houses, got rid of his fields, and built that rocky eyrie up on the castle rock, living like a cuckoo, and caring to see neither Christian nor Turk, until some years later he died, and in his will left a blessing,

for it bade the people use his money to supply
the village with water, so that now his soul is
blessed by priests and imams alike? What
was it brought all this woe upon him, if not
his mother's curse?

PRINTED BY
TURNBULL AND SPEARS
EDINBURGH